FREE FOR ALL

A Lexi Fagan Mystery

Autumn Doerr

This book is a work of fiction. The characters, with the exception of Stella Brooks, are made up. Stella Brooks was a real person with a wry sense of humor whom Autumn Doerr knew when she lived in San Francisco in the 1980s. Brooks was a jazz singer and performed at the Purple Onion in the 1940s with some of the greats. Please look her up at Smithsonian Folkways Records. Stella Brooks is here in spirit; although her words on these pages were never uttered, Ms. Doerr wishes to honor her memory. Any other resemblance to actual persons, living or dead, actual events and locations is a coincidence.

Kindle ISBN 978-0-9861209-3-0
WGA Registration 2031754
© Copyright 2019, Autumn Doerr
All rights reserved.

ISBN-10: 0986120928
ISBN-13: 978-0986120923
Library of Congress Control Number: 2019655042
Autumn Doerr, Pasadena, CA

Cover by Jenny Mikesell
Author photograph by Josh Fogel

To my dearest Doerrs,
Suzanne and Heather.

"Every real argument is a murder,"

Arthur Miller

(From "Arthur Miller: Writer" documentary

by filmmaker Rebecca Miller, HBO, 2018)

TABLE OF CONTENTS

1

THURSDAY, OCTOBER 17,

1985—HE'S DEAD

Juanita Theresa Luisa Gomez emptied the wastebasket near the reception desk at The Freedom Institute. It was Thursday at 2:30 a.m. There would be one more office to clean before heading home at 3:00. She felt a twinge in her back as she bent down to return the basket under the desk.

Outside the last office before the bathrooms, Juanita polished the brass plaque.

David F. Emerson III

President, The Freedom Institute

"He moves fastest who moves alone."—Milton Friedman

She turned the knob, but the door was locked. Taking the master key ring from her pocket, she unlocked the door, pushed it open and moved her cleaning cart into the room. The dim desk lamp was lit, but most of the employees at the Institute left their lights on.

Juanita switched on the overhead lights and parked the vacuum in the corner. She would wait to vacuum until the dusting and trash collecting were finished. She had strict orders never to touch anyone's desks. Not that she cared what was on them, she was glad to leave them alone. People were touchy about their things.

She rounded the desk and stopped short. A pair of legs stretched out from underneath at an odd angle, the shoulders and head were under the desk. She put one hand to her mouth and the other to her heart. She stared at the black socks exposed below the pants that were twisted around the legs.

"Mr. David?" she whispered, clutching her blouse tighter.

Juanita was a fan of detective novels and knew better than to touch anything at the scene of an accident or a crime. But what if the killer were still in the office? She slowly backed out of the room, walked quickly out of the Institute offices and down the hall. She let herself into the recruitment firm on the same floor, picked up the phone on the reception desk and dialed 911, still holding her breath until she heard the calm voice of the dispatcher.

"911. What is your emergency?"

"There is a dead person under Mr. David's desk." Her English was good, but she spoke slowly because of her accent. She answered the dispatcher's questions: No, she didn't know who it was but suspected it was Mr. David. No, she hadn't checked to see if he was alive, because he was dead. No, she didn't see anyone. She was the cleaning lady. Yes, she would let the police in the building.

Juanita gave the address, hung up the phone and took the elevator to the lobby to wait for the police.

An hour later, the investigation team had nearly finished dusting for prints and collecting evidence. Juanita had been questioned and sent home. Pictures had been taken of the position of the desk before moving it to expose the body underneath. It was 3:45 a.m.

Outside the office windows, the streets were wet. Fog obscured the large office towers with shops along the Embarcadero across the street. Detective Robert Reiger was watching Dr. Yu examine the body. Reiger's dark skin glowed from sweat and residual rain.

"Is the heater on in here?" he asked of no one in particular. Taking out a handkerchief, he wiped his brow and turned to Yu.

Anticipating his question, Yu said, "Died about midnight, give or take."

"Age?"

"Mid-30s." Yu's plastic raincoat squeaked as he stood next to Reiger, who was taller and huskier than Yu, a lean and wiry 80-year-old.

They looked down at the body. It was face down with the head turned on its side. The temples were streaked with gray. Reiger gave Yu a look.

"He's not prematurely graying." Yu laughed. "That's a dye job."

Reiger shrugged, "To each his own." He took off his rumpled raincoat and draped it over his arm.

Yu stared at Reiger's leather jacket. "Gift from the wife?"

Reiger nodded. "Jackie was getting tired of the 'Black Columbo" rap I get from the media."

"From Columbo to Shaft." Yu smiled. "I'm sure that Columbo shit gets old just like the "you" jokes I get." Reiger returned the smile.

He pointed his pencil toward the wall. "Let's get back to Columbo-ing. Looks like there's been a struggle." The chair was on its side and there was a black smudge mark under the window behind the desk that looked out onto Front Street. "Looks like the chair's been shoved away from the desk." Yu nodded.

Blood had pooled under the victim's head and oozed into the Persian carpet.

"Bet you wish you'd stayed retired?" Reiger teased.

Yu leaned over the body and scraped vomit from around the corpse's mouth, open in a ghoulish silent howl. "It's quite the opposite," Yu said. "You know, it's my job to answer for the dead who can't speak for themselves." Reiger smiled. Yu tended to rhapsodize about life and death. It was familiar and comforting.

Yu put the crusty liquid into a vial.

Reiger asked. "I wonder how he ended up under the desk?"

"It's quite a trajectory," Dr. Yu said. "I'll know more when I get him on the slab. If I had to bet—." Yu took the pointer he was holding and moved a bloody clump of hair exposing a pool of blood under the skin. "Hit his head on the wall." He looked at Reiger, who nodded.

"Besides, why would I want to stay in retirement and take care of my 100-year-old mother who"—here Yu imitated his stern mother's voice—"can take care of myself, thank you very much!" Yu dropped the accent and smiled, showing his teeth. "When I could be working a murder case with you?"

"Sergeant Stryker might get me to retire early."

"That guy," Yu said. "His claim to fame is failing upward. Three strikes and Stryker's in, not out." Looking at the forensic team working the room, Yu leaned closer to Reiger and whispered. "He's never liked you."

"I've never liked him."

"How did you get this juicy case?" Yu looked puzzled.

"Beats me, but he's not going to stop me from solving this one."

Yu shook his head. "1977." Reiger took a deep breath to shake off the memory of the case that got away.

They turned back to the body. Reiger said, "Maybe he was struck with such force that his chair rolled back against the wall and he hit his head." Reiger reenacted the scene. "He staggered out of the chair, onto his knees and—," he paused. "Then what? Crawled under the desk and died?"

"I don't think so." Dr. Yu motioned for Reiger to return to the dead man's head, took his pointer again and lifted a piece of hair in another location, exposing a chunk of missing scalp. "See that missing bit? There's a missing piece to this puzzle."

Reiger looked around the floor for the piece.

Yu continued, "The weapon was sharp and pointed and took part of his head with it."

Addressing the tech team sweeping the room for clues, Reiger said, "Has anyone seen a sharp object with bits of head on it?" They stopped dusting and bagging and looked at Reiger, shaking their heads, unsure how to react. "Nothing, Sir."

The highest-ranking officer on the forensic team, Linda Corbin, laughed. The two men in the room were fresh recruits; no doubt they were included to throw Reiger off balance by his boss, Detective Sergeant Emanuel Stryker. Reiger saw the men look at each other for guidance. He gave Linda a knowing look. She had logged a lot of hours working with Reiger and Yu.

Reiger moved to the door and pulled it closed. Examining the door, Reiger noticed a portion of missing wood near the top. "The hook's gone. It's been ripped off probably with the jacket or coat." He addressed the team, "Did any of you find this hook?"

"No, Detective."

"How about a suit jacket or overcoat?"

"No, Sir."

He picked up a date book sitting open on the desk, his gloved finger pointing to a date. "This is what was supposed to happen today." He read the entry for October 17th, "12:30 p.m., Mary, one-month anniversary."

Yu pointed to a photo of a young mother with twin babies on the desk. "One-month anniversary of what? These babies are at least a year and change. Anniversary implies something intimate. Could this Mary be a lover?"

"Interesting." Reiger looked at Linda, who was dusting for prints, then looked at his watch. "Are you close to wrapping this up? I need a cup of strong tea before I track down the loved ones."

"Not long now." Linda continued to brush the glass on the desk. "I sent one of the guys to the bathroom looking for vomit. There's nothing in the garbage cans."

"Pretty gruesome." Reiger looked at Yu. "You know what that means? Start looking at the family." They both laughed. Linda smiled at the gallows humor as she packed the ink and brushes into the kit on the floor next to the desk.

"Family." Yu looked up. "You can't live with 'em and you can't kill 'em. If my mother doesn't croak soon, I tell her it'll be pillow-over-the-face-time."

Reiger patted Yu on the shoulder and chuckled. "Glad to have you back."

The color of the carpet and walls of The Freedom Institute were burgundy and black accented in pale pink. Reiger said, "I don't know who decided these colors screamed 'Freedom.'" Two of the walls were lined with bookshelves. He read the titles to Yu. "*The American Century, How Capitalism will Save the World,* and get this, Yu,

You and Libertarianism." He saw a copy of *Atlas Shrugged* and took it from the shelf. Ayn Rand's signature was on the title page. "A signed first edition."

"It's not that old." Yu said. "Wasn't she writing in the '50s? That's only, what, 30 years ago?"

Reiger scanned a few pages. "1957."

Yu asked, "How'd you know it was a first edition? Wait. I remember. You're a book guy."

Reiger smiled and picked up a copy of *The Fountainhead* from David's desk. He opened the copyright page and pointed to a set of numbers. "See that number one?"

Yu looked at the numbers "10 9 8 7 6 5 4 3 2 1." "Yeah? And?"

"That number 'one' means it's a first edition, but also here." He put that book down and picked up the *Atlas Shrugged*, turning to the copyright page. The top line read "First Printing."

"Very funny." Yu laughed. "You got me there, Detective."

Reiger set the book back on the shelf and turned his attention to the credenza. There were a dozen or so framed photographs of Emerson with politicians and businessmen. Reiger recognized two of the people in the pictures: Henry Kissinger and the economist Milton Friedman. He picked up the only photograph with an African American. He was seated at a table in a ballroom behind David Emerson, captured mid-shake with a man he recognized, a famous body builder.

One photo in the corner was of David sitting at his desk holding an Institute newsletter, smiling proudly. Reiger took it out of the frame and put it in his pocket.

He turned to Yu and asked. "Did you notice the name on the reception desk?"

"Not unless there was a dead body next to it. Details without a body are your department."

"Lexi Fagan." Yu's face was blank. Reiger continued, "The redhead from the bakery." There was still no sign of recognition. "It was a couple years ago; the fire at the Cathedral Hill Hotel where they found Jerry Stevens' body. The firefighter. His girlfriend, Lexi." Reiger paused. "Nothing?"

"Oh, yeah. Strangulation then fire. Whoever killed him planted the body during the hotel fire hoping it would burn up. Fascinating. They put a beam over his throat like it had crushed his neck, but what they didn't know was that the damage to the strap muscles can't be covered up."

Reiger knew there was more information coming and waited. There was nothing like a dead body to animate Yu.

"The ligature underneath the skin in the neck. The killer pushed so hard he crushed the trachea on both sides. A crushed trachea from a beam would occur only on contact. Since the body hadn't burned completely, the bruising and tearing to the muscle tissue was visible in two areas. The life and death of the muscle could still be read. We caught the bastard, right?"

Reiger nodded. "Both of them."

Dr. Yu pulled a cigarette from a half-empty pack and put it behind his ear. "Now I remember her, Miss Fagan. She came into the morgue with my old PI friend, Henry. For someone who'd never seen a dead body before, she was pretty strong. She looked at her boyfriend's burned face and didn't even throw up like most of my first-years."

One of the newbies came into the office and whispered something to Linda. She turned to Reiger. "Turns out there were specks of vomit in the toilet. We bagged it." Reiger stared to follow Linda out of the office, but stopped and turned to Yu. "Lexi's a good kid. She reminds me of my Jada." Reiger regretted the comparison between his daughter and Lexi as soon as the words left his mouth.

Yu frowned. "What are the chances she would show up on another murder case?" Yu didn't look up from David's rigid face, his dead eyes staring at the ceiling.

2

LEXI FAGAN

It was mid-October. Leaves scattered the tree-lined sidewalks. The rain had turned back to dense fog, smudging the air and clinging to the ground. Lexi drank her cappuccino and watch as people scurried outside the window of the Cigar Store Café. A few old men wearing fedoras and wool suits drank their cappuccinos over a heated conversation in Italian. She had lost her enthusiasm for walking to work. Her hair curled its way out of her ponytail as she pushed it away from her damp face.

She turned her attention to Washington Square Park and Saints Peter & Paul Church beyond. It was where Jerry's funeral had taken place. She heard a bus coming up the street, downed the remains of her drink and grabbed her book-bag to make a run for it. It was a 35 Stockton, a local, not routed to downtown. Lexi slowed her pace and walked to the nearest bus stop to wait for the next one.

The wind was pushing its way down Union Street and seemed to cut right through her. It carried a particular North Beach scent of wet pavement and roasted coffee beans, like burned toast.

At the bus shelter, she tightened her scarf around her neck and watched as people darted in and out of the rain. She had lived in San Francisco long enough to find the best vintage clothing stores. Her wardrobe had morphed from jeans and oversized sweaters to men's suit jackets, pencil skirts worn with bright-colored tights and discarded bowling shoes her boyfriend said smelled of feet and antiseptic spray.

Had it only been two years since Jerry died? After the convictions of Jerry's killers, Lexi had quit the bakery for an office job downtown. She still missed McCracken's. Mostly it was the friends who had helped her when Jerry went missing and, later, when he turned up dead.

There was the former private eye, Henry, who taught her that inconsistencies are often clues. Stella, a jazz singer in her younger days who forced Lexi to toughen up and, finally, Tiny Timm whose crooked spine and immobile legs made every day a challenge. He had a sunny nature despite his disabilities that helped her put things into perspective. She was glad they still got together at regular poker nights.

Since they had become close because of Jerry, their closeness was sometimes bittersweet. Each of them reminded her of him, her first love. She marveled that her closest friendships had come out of tragedy, but these misfits had accepted her and guided her at her most vulnerable stages of grief.

The 41 Union pulled over. Lexi climbed on board, along with a few office workers and a Chinese grandmother. She had a baby cradled on her belly, wrapped in colorfully printed cloth slung around her shoulder and she pushed her way through the crowd like a linebacker. Lexi spied an open seat and followed in the grandmother's wake. The last of the self-defense classes that Lexi had taken the night before made her body sore and her arm hurt when she bumped into a passenger.

Seated, she put on her earphones. The aria "Un bel di vedremo," from "Madama Butterfly" played on her Walkman. She watched the Italian cafés, bars, delis, and pizza places with tattered curtains in the upper windows pass by. The Condor Club and other topless bars appeared at Broadway, followed by Tosca Café and, across the street, Café Vesuvio next to City Lights Books and then Brandy Ho's Hunan as the bus passed Chinatown at Pacific Street.

The hill flattened and the colorful sights of North Beach gave way to high-rise office buildings towering over the street that had turned from Columbus Avenue into Montgomery Street. The corner with the Transamerica Pyramid was like a talisman marking the entrance to the Financial District.

For as small as San Francisco's 46 square miles were, this part of town felt like new territory for Lexi to explore. It was as if the years she had worked at McCracken's Bakery on Van Ness were a lifetime ago and a world away.

Like most rainy days that lend to melancholy, Lexi brooded over Jerry and felt guilty that she thought more about him than she did of Cosmo. To bring him back into her heart, she replayed in her mind the first time she visited Cosmo on his houseboat, the Sea Worthy, in Sausalito.

Sausalito was like the movie set of a seaside village, what Lexi's hometown of Ketchikan might look like if it were in California and had a larger population. Houses dotted the hills surrounding the bay, their picture windows partially obscured by trees. Instead of Alaskan fishing boats with gear and netting, the harbor was crowded with clean white boats and blue tarps strung with lights along the masts.

Lexi often thought that Sausalito was made up of two towns. There was the one with homes worth hundreds of thousands of dollars perched above the shopping district, filled with tourists. The San Francisco skyline gleamed in the distance like Oz.

At the other end of town, near the freeway across from Marin City, was another harbor of makeshift houseboats along a faded pier. This was where hippies, dropouts and back-to-nature types raised shoeless kids, ate organic food and built top-heavy floating structures that had never seen a code enforcer. The skyline across the bay was the same for the rich as for the poor.

That first day at the funky end of town, Lexi had walked the pier giddy with anticipation as she admired the character and creativity of the place. She had spotted the Sea Worthy. The small boat bobbed gently in its slip. She had cried out with surprise at the homemade sign that read, "Welcome Lexi!"

"Ahoy!" Lexi yelled as she clumsily stepped over the side of the houseboat and landed on the deck with a thud.

She remembered Cosmo appearing from below deck, "Did you just say 'Ahoy?'" His long, straight blonde hair had been pulled into a ponytail; his beard obscured the dimples of his smiling face.

"I'm getting used to nautical terms." She had tried not to rock the boat as she stood. "I believe that's from 'Gilligan's Island,'" she had said before kissing him hello.

"You're a nut. Come inside. I've made lunch."

She and Cosmo had been dating for three months, but a living, breathing man was no competition for the boyfriend she had lost so soon after they had fallen for each other. She tried to hide it from Cosmo, but Lexi was unable to let go of her first true love. She still felt the sting when Cosmo made it clear how he felt about how Lexi dwelled on Jerry. After one month of dating, he said, "Yeah, I know. It was a magical date." The sarcasm was not lost on her.

Lexi's mind snapped back. Her reverie of Cosmo and Sausalito was broken as the bus lurched to the curb.

While David Emerson's body was cooling in an icy drawer in the city morgue, Detective Reiger caught a few winks in his car while waiting for McCracken's Bakery to open at 7:00 a.m. He had started taking tea breaks there during the Stevens case where he had first met Lexi. Reiger liked checking in with the rank and file cops hanging out there, and the bakery had a city vibe he appreciated. Drug addicts from the methadone clinic and retired ladies from the dilapidated Art Deco apartments in the Tenderloin District mingled with tourists at McCracken's. To Reiger, that's what made the city the city.

He had lost track of Lexi after she had left the bakery, but that was what happened once a case was closed, the trial was over and the files stored in a metal cabinet in the office.

Reiger saw Claudia unlock the front door. He got out of the car, locked the door and greeted her as she motioned for him to enter the bakery. The lights flickered on as he took a seat. She set an empty cup on the table and fetched the steaming coffee pot.

"Coffee, Officer?" Claudia held the pot over his cup. He mused, as he often did, that her Russian accent was as thick as her fingers that held the handle in a death grip.

"Tea, please. And, Claudia, I'm not an officer, remember? I'm a detective."

This misunderstanding was a dance they performed at every visit.

"Ah," Claudia said as if Reiger had affirmed that he, indeed, was a beat cop.

She poured and delivered the tea along with his usual bear claw before slipping behind the front counter.

It was getting on 7:45 a.m. and Reiger wanted to be at The Freedom Institute offices before the staff showed up. As he stood to leave, he wondered, again, what Yu had said at the crime scene; what were the odds that Lexi Fagan would be working at the scene of another murder?

Lexi was the first to arrive in the office every morning at 8:30 a.m. She made a point never to be late. The coffee cup in Julia's office had a different kind of dregs, a detail Lexi wanted to keep hidden from the rest of the office. She was loyal because Julia had hired her even though she had had no office experience. Her work history consisted of the summer job at an old folks' home before her senior year of high school and the two years she had been with McCracken's Bakery. Lexi had answered an ad in the paper for a receptionist position and felt lucky that Julia had given her the job. It wasn't until later that Lexi thought it might have been to Julia's advantage to hire an ally.

3

THE FREEDOM INSTITUTE

Someone pulled the cord for Sacramento Street, and Lexi turned off her Walkman. The murmuring of Italian and Cantonese filled the air as she got off the bus. She walked the remaining blocks to her office above The Royal Exchange Bar at Front and Sacramento.

She could smell urine as she approached the heavy doors to the building. Once inside, she rode the elevator to the third floor, stepped off and rounded the corner to The Freedom Institute offices. The door was open. Panicked that she might be late, she ran through the open door, right into Detective Reiger.

"Detective Reiger!" she exclaimed as he steadied her on her feet.

Reiger stepped back. Lexi looked about the same. Even though her hair was matted from the fog, it was still curly and red, though dark from the wet day. There was the familiar book-bag that looked like it would pull her over. Only her clothes were different. Less Alaska and more San Francisco. "Lexi, here we are again."

"Hello, Detective. Has there been a murder?" Lexi laughed, not expecting to hear a "yes," but Reiger wasn't smiling.

"You'd better sit down." Lexi sat heavily behind the reception desk. She twisted the soggy ends of her hair into a knot at the base of her neck.

Reiger leaned against the wall. Four hours had passed between the time that the crime scene team had wrapped up and now. The fluorescent lights were still on, overpowering the desk lamps. The flat light made the office look shabby. The gilded-framed paintings of dark landscapes and Persian rugs looked dull and wanting.

Reiger said, "David Emerson's dead." Lexi was at a loss for words. He continued, "The cleaning woman found him early this morning."

"Oh! Poor Juanita."

Reiger gave Lexi the rundown of how the body was found.

She let the news sink in. "How did it happen? I mean, how did he die?"

"I'll get to that later." He gave her a crooked smile. "You know how this works. Were you close to Mr. Emerson?"

"No." Lexi felt numb. "We never talked about anything but work."

"Can you think of anyone who had a grudge against him? Someone who wanted to hurt him?"

"I can't imagine anyone wanting him dead." She paused trying to take in the news. "Although he did recently leave his wife for a rich donor. And five years ago he left the Reed Foundation with half their donors to start TFI." She motioned to the offices down the hall.

Reiger gave Lexi a look. She said, "The Freedom Institute, TFI. It's a libertarian think tank, but as far as I can tell, thinking isn't high on their list." She was regaining her composure. "They're smart but sometimes they act like spoiled babies."

Reiger looked sideways. "And you know every libertarian and can say with confidence they are spoiled babies?" he smiled.

"I think that is the dictionary definition," Lexi said as she smiled weakly.

"You would point the finger to David's former employers or his wife. Might be a crime of passion."

Lexi nodded. She and Detective Reiger had history. Trying to figure out what had happened to Jerry two years earlier, Lexi and the detective had become unlikely collaborators.

Reiger leaned on the desk and looked at the computer that took up most of the surface. There was a desk blotter, a cup filled with pens and a stack of papers in a slot marked "In Box."

"Is there anything going on at work that would push someone over the edge?"

"I don't know. Libertarians are passionate about their ideas. I've heard rumors about a book that a big donor paid for that hasn't been written.

Lexi thought for a moment. "Mr. Emerson's been distracted with the separation and his girl-friend, so not much is getting done. He's well connected. We have four big fundraisers a year and book parties. We have a lot of donors."

"That's quite a long list. Help me narrow it down so I don't have to interview the entire city."

"Do you know about libertarians?" she asked.

"Let me ask the questions, young lady." It was a good-natured comment. "How long have you worked here?"

"It's been over a year."

Reiger looked around the reception area. There were tall shelves with books with identical looking spines, a burgundy couch, two burgundy chairs and a coffee table crammed into the space in front of the reception desk. "Are these the books the Institute puts out?"

Lexi nodded.

He looked at his watch. "What time do people come to work around here?"

Lexi said, "Anywhere from nine-thirty to ten o'clock."

"Ten. That's unusual for an office."

"Libertarians." Lexi smiled. "I tried to tell you."

"I know about libertarianism." Reiger's face went still before he smiled.

Lexi blushed.

Reiger continued. "Every young man reads Ayn Rand's *Atlas Shrugged* in college as part of their misspent youth. Anyway, we don't have time for economic theory. Before people start rolling in here, give me the lowdown on the staff." Reiger moved from his perch on the desk to the couch. His stiff leather jacket relaxed as he sat. "Did anyone have a grudge against Mr. Emerson?"

"It's more like who didn't." Lexi looked around as if someone might overhear. "David wasn't popular."

"He's dead, Lexi. And there's no one here yet."

"It's hard to get that through my head." She reached into her desk drawer and pulled out a pair of glasses from its box. "These are Mr. Emerson's glasses." She walked around the desk and handed them to Reiger. "Put them on."

He hesitated for a moment before putting them on. He had a big head. "They don't fit, but I can see."

"Exactly," Lexi said triumphant. "They're plain glass. No corrective lenses. Mr. Emerson is obsessed with appearances. He wants to look older. He's only 36." She stopped. "I mean he was only 36."

"That explains it. Dr. Yu noticed Mr. Emerson's temples were dyed gray."

"I knew it!" Lexi said. Reiger took the glasses off, shook out a small padded envelope he took from his pocket and put the glasses inside before returning it to his pocket. "Evidence."

"Now," said Lexi. "You want to know who Mr. Emerson's enemies were. Who had motive and opportunity?"

Reiger smiled. "Sometime today. Why do you call him Mr. Emerson?"

"I always called him that. Everyone else called him David, but—" she paused. "David liked the receptionist to keep things formal."

She pulled a staff list with phone extensions from the desk drawer and handed it to him. The first name was Julia Collins, followed by Renée Samuelson. The list was organized by extension number.

"Julia is the office manager." Here she hesitated. "She hired me and we're close. She was okay with Mr.—" she corrected herself, "David." Lexi didn't tell Reiger about the wine in the coffee cup. Her loyalty ran deep. Every position at the

Institute required a college degree, but Julia had overlooked it.

Lexi started to feel uneasy. It was sinking in. Could one of her coworkers have killed Mr. Emerson? Could it be Julia? She remembered many lunches when Julia had hinted that their boss had done things that could implicate her also. Lexi hadn't taken it seriously.

She ran down the list of employees in her mind, trying to eliminate them as suspects before remembering another person. "Gretchen Stenholm. She owns hotels. She lost her husband at about the time I started working here. I don't know why she rents offices from the Institute, but that's her door at the end of the hall."

Reiger made a note before moving to the next name on the list. "What's your take on Renée?"

"She handles the authors."

Reiger looked up.

"What we mostly do here is raise money from business leaders to publish books about how libertarian theory applies to whatever business they're in. Renée is the go-between between the writers and David."

"Are there that many books?"

"Oh, yes. We publish about ten books a year." She reached into a drawer and pulled out a newsletter. Reiger flipped through it. There were books with long descriptions on every page.

Reiger asked. "Anything else about Renée?"

"I'm not proud of this, but we make fun of her behind her back, about how she talks. She qualifies everything she says. She'll say, 'Here's what I'm going to say' or 'This is what I'll say about that.'"

"That says something about you and not her, don't you think?" It wasn't a question. "Anything else?"

Lexi's cheeks reddened. "Well, she's always on me because she knows I didn't go to college. I hate to admit it, but it gets under my skin." Reiger's steady look made Lexi squirm. She said, "And that also says something about me and not Renée." She paused. "She's married to one of the Clark brothers. Oil money." Reiger nodded.

Lexi continued, "It makes her the queen of the castle round here."

"Then I'm sure David had to like her," Reiger chuckled. "How does Renée feel about David?"

"She worships him. She has pictures of him with the big donors in her office. Her husband's front and center. They're like book ends in her collection of powerful men."

"Who's next?" Reiger took up his pencil.

"There's Peggy Neville. She's a copy editor, but she has a heavy hand. She's rumored to rewrite some of the worst writers."

"This is getting better and better."

"Well, according to Julia, the academics that write these kinds of things are incredibly boring, and David has his own ideas of how the theory applies to the real world. I couldn't tell you what they are. Even after Peggy gives the books a once-over, they're still too dense for me."

Rain started a steady beat against the window.

"Peggy and David?"

"She got along with David. The thing about Peggy is that she's barely on the planet. She's super smart but she's an absent-minded professor type. She's always kind of a mess. You know, wearing the same suit for a week and not even changing her blouse. Her husband is a rare book dealer. They're both brainiacs with no common sense. His name's Grey."

Reiger sat up. "Grey Neville?"

"Yeah. Do you know him?"

"He's well known. I see him around the East Bay at Moe's and Pendragon books. How many rare book dealers who are black do you think there are in this area?"

Lexi stared at Reiger.

"You're not going to be surprised I buy old books, are you?"

"No. It's not that. I just don't know anything about you." She didn't want to admit that she was surprised.

"Let's stick to the subject, your dead boss. Are you close to—" Reiger glanced at the staff list, —"Jack?"

Before Lexi could answer, the door opened and Renée walked in. Her raven hair was coiffed into feathered perfection, her neat suit and pumps dry. A well put-together professional. She stopped and seemed to pose as she looked at Reiger. Lexi could see she had the same regard for him as she did everyone, a combination of disdain and impatience.

"And you are—" Renée hesitated before extending her hand.

"Detective Robert Reiger, San Francisco Homicide."

"Renée Samuelson, author relations." Her cold expression was steady. "It's David, isn't it?"

"How do you know about Mr. Emerson?" Reiger asked.

"*Is* it David?" Renée's demeanor changed. She set her briefcase on the coffee table and put her hand to her mouth.

"It is. I'm afraid he's gone." He moved to escort her to the couch as she collapsed.

Lexi said, "I know how much you respected him."

"I do." Renée paused, a slight catch in her voice. "I did."

Reiger said, "I'll need to speak with you later, but you should go home until someone in my office notifies you. Is there someone who can pick you up?"

Lexi looked at Renée. She was married to one of the richest men in the U.S.

Reiger showed Renée the phone list. "Is this your current home number?" She nodded.

Renée had Lexi call for a car. Before she left the office, Renée stopped. "The fundraiser is tomorrow night!"

Reiger waited for her to explain. "Here's what I'm going to say about that. It's our big donor night at the Fairmont. And, it's too late to cancel." She was lost in thought.

Addressing Lexi, Reiger whispered, "Is she serious?"

"Serious as a guillotine."

Renée ignored them and turned back into the crisp professional woman who had walked into the office. "Lexi. Tell the staff we're moving ahead as planned. I want everyone at the hotel an hour before dinner. Wicked Smith has an engagement, so, I'll tell you this, you'll need to arrange the book table and check in the guests."

Lexi looked from Reiger to Renée. "What do we tell the donors about David?"

"That he's dead." Renée picked up her briefcase, turned and walked out.

"That was weird." Lexi said. "Did you notice how dry she was? Not a drop."

Reiger stood and walked to the desk. "I had noticed that, detective," he said, giving her a nod. "Let's get through this list before they show up." He raised an eyebrow. "Wicked Smith?"

"That's the name of his band. I don't know what his real name is. We call him Wicked."

"I'd like to see the details on the fundraiser." Lexi looked through the papers in the In Box and took out an invitation. Reiger looked it over before he put it in his other pocket.

"How many people are employed at The Freedom Institute?"

"Well, there's Renée, Julia, Peggy—she also writes all the book proposals on top of writing the books. Jack Abbott. He's PR. Me. Mr. Emerson. Who am I missing?"

Just then, the door swung open and Jack—the only employee in the PR department, but a man insecure enough to insist on being called the "director." His suit was heavily rumpled and his hair matted down and wet. Ignoring Reiger, Jack turned to Lexi. "Did I get a package?"

"It's nine o'clock." She looked from Jack to Reiger. "Jack. This is Detective Reiger. Something has happened. There's news." Lexi reached into her desk drawer for a paper towel and handed it to Jack. He wiped his face and patted his hair.

"Well, news is my business." Jack stuck out his hand. "Jack Abbott. I'm in charge of public relations, the director, to be precise." When Reiger didn't react, Jack continued to clarify. "You know press releases, publicity for books, newsy stuff. What's up?"

Reiger slowly shook Jack's hand. "You might want to sit down for this kind of news."

Jack stepped to the couch and sat down, sprawling across the cushions.

"David Emerson is dead."

"What?" Jack jumped up. Lexi couldn't tell if he was sweating or still wet from the rain.

"Does that mean the office is closing? I'm expecting a package."

"Jack! What is wrong with you?" Lexi asked. "David is dead."

"Dead how? Heart attack—wait, murder? I bet he was murdered. I say follow the money. David could sense money like blood in the water." He gave Lexi a pleading look. She shook her head. No package.

"Where were you last night?" Reiger asked.

"Oh me?" Jack grinned like a naughty schoolboy. "Out on a date. Sorry, Lex. I can't wait forever for my redhead."

"You don't seem upset to hear your boss has died." Reiger looked at Lexi as she scooted her chair for a better view of Jack, a moving target.

"No. No. Terribly upset." Jack's hands swept the room. He dropped the wet paper towels on the coffee table. "I'm devastated. In a state of shock, old man."

"I'll need the name of your date," Reiger said. "How late were you out, old man?" Jack's smile faded as he looked at Reiger. His tone softened. "Until about an hour ago."

4

JULIA COLLINS

Detective Reiger told Lexi he would contact the remaining staff about David. She needed to talk with Julia. When she had reached her by phone, Julia's reaction to the news was peculiar. She asked no questions about how or when David had died. She insisted on coming to the office, but that was impossible since Reiger had made it clear no one was to come in.

Once Lexi had assured Julia that she would bring the guest list for the fundraiser, she had calmed down, requesting now they meet for lunch. The thought of food made Lexi realize that she was starved. Retrieving the list, she said goodbye to Detective Reiger and caught the 38 Geary bus.

Julia had suggested Benihana in Japantown near Geary and Webster. Though it was an area she tried to avoid, Lexi had agreed. The restaurant was close to the Cathedral Hill Hotel, where Jerry's body had been found. Memories of his burned face haunted her. The hotel had recently reopened and was often written about in the *San Francisco Chronicle*.

At the restaurant, Julia had taken a table away from where the chefs' knives flew over an open flame. Despite the dim light, Lexi could see the strain on Julia's face. Her brown hair and tasteful blonde highlights were not as neat as usual. Rings gleamed on her manicured fingers. There was a large bow at the neck of her silk blouse. Her pencil skirt was all business. She was 15 years older than Lexi, but looked much older. The smoking didn't help.

Lexi declined the glass of wine Julia had ordered for her. Julia's approval was important to her so she tread lightly. She asked, "Is there something I should know about David?" Julia shook her head no.

"Nothing from his time at Reed?" She took a deep breath before continuing. "You have hinted a few times that David could implicate you somehow."

Julia scoffed. "That was the wine talking." She raised her glass, lost in thought. "We were so idealistic when we started. David cared about everything. Objectivism, the whole world-view. Even

Jack felt that way. He wrote passionate editorials. I don't remember when it changed."

Lexi had wanted confirmation that Julia had no motive to kill David. She tried to accept Julia's reassurance, but was not entirely convinced.

5

HOME

At home, Lexi retrieved a message on her answering machine from Cosmo setting their call for 6:30 p.m. He drove an ambulance on the day shift. Scheduled phone calls were their only means of communication during the week. Their habit was to talk every other night at a set time, until the weekend.

They had made plans to see "Jagged Edge" at Cinema 21 in the Marina on Saturday, but Lexi knew she couldn't sit through a movie. Once they had made a plan, they tended to stick to it since there was no phone on the boat and Lexi didn't own a car.

They changed their plans. On Friday they would make an appearance at the Institute fundraiser where Lexi would set up the book table before heading to Berkeley and their favorite dance club. They would return to stay at Lexi's on Larkin Street in the city, then roller skate in Golden Gate Park on Saturday before heading across the bridge to the Sea Worthy. Their plans tended to include a lot of back and forth across bridges and bays, as overly complex plans can be when you're young.

Thursday at 6:30 p.m. sharp Cosmo would be waiting at the phone booth near the dock to check in. She dialed and he answered. Before he could say "hello," Lexi blurted out that her boss had been killed.

"I saw the call log for an ambulance," Cosmo said. "I've been worried. Are you okay?"

"I think I'm still in shock, but I'm fine."

Lexi thought that dancing the following night would distract her from brooding. David's death reminded her of Jerry's, and that took her back to losing her parents when she was still a baby. She felt as if she were waking from a long dream. It was best to stay active and Cosmo was the right guy if you wanted to keep busy. They said goodbye, having firmed up their plans.

Luckily, tonight was her regular poker game. She would have to tell her bakery friends about David. His death would be covered in the *Chronicle* in the morning.

The longer she worked at The Freedom Institute, the less she saw of her old friends. Losing touch with them made her feel as if she were abandoning Jerry too. She felt a familiar twinge of loneliness.

Moving to San Francisco had been an escape from the claustrophobia Lexi had felt in her hometown. It wasn't the physical place that constrained her, but there had been no place to hide from her parent's tragic death or the pity of well-meaning family and friends. She often heard the story of how June and Max had met at the Klondike Bar. Max had knocked out a rival's teeth defending June's honor. It wasn't until she entered high school that Lexi noticed no one told stories about her parents after they had met. As if they were sealed in amber at that bar. She imagined them swashbuckling around the Alaskan panhandle in their seaplane, dropping supplies to an expedition, carrying medical kits to an outpost or rescuing a wounded sled dog.

The lack of stories was surprising. Ketchikan ran on gossip, fishing and crabbing, a pulp mill and, more recently, oil. Clusters of fishing boats dotted the water or were berthed at the docks along the narrows. Lexi found the scent of tar and motor oil comforting. She often visited Fisherman's Wharf to get a whiff of home.

To outsiders there wasn't that much to see. Besides the totem pole park, Saxman Bite, the landmark that Lexi's cat had been named after, tourists shuffled off cruise ships covered in rain gear and visited Dolly's House, named for a famous madam who thrived on Creek Street during the gold rush. Lexi's favorite place in Ketchikan, as it was in San Francisco, was the library. It was where she escaped downcast eyes and the tut-tutting of people who felt sorry for her.

It's not that Doris and Brody weren't kind grandparents. They were ham-fisted, don't-tread-on-me eccentrics. Lexi learned to play poker during their regular games on summer afternoons. Often, after too many Scotch and Cokes, one of their friends would pick up a rifle, run outside and shoot at a passing raven, scaring Saxman half to death.

The truth was that her grandparents embarrassed her. She preferred the sophistication of San Franciscans where the eccentrics were charming. Like the identical twins, Vivian and Marian Brown, extravagantly dressed in matching fur hats and coats. Everything they wore mirrored the other down to the hairdos, make-up and handbags. She loved the Italian men knocking over chess pieces and waving cigars during heated conversations in Washington Square.

It seemed to Lexi that the hangover from San Francisco's gold rush had softened into a bohemian watercolor. She preferred that image to the rough edges of Ketchikan, where a tinge of boom and bust still ran through it like a depleted vein of gold.

Except for the two murders, Lexi mused. Those weren't exactly watercolors.

As expected, the phone rang. She picked it up.

"Lexi?! Lexi?!" Doris was yelling into the phone.

"I'm here, Gram." Lexi talked a little about Cosmo but said nothing of the drama that had consumed her life.

"You made short work of him," Doris said.

"What do you mean?" Lexi was perplexed. Sometimes Doris confused Jerry with Cosmo and Lexi hoped it wouldn't be necessary to straighten her out.

Doris repeated, "You made short work of him." There was no getting to the bottom of that thought. Lexi needed to get off the phone and on her way to the Sunset District. Luckily, Doris changed the subject to Brody's arthritis and his bad heart before landing on what she wanted to talk about. It was an old grievance with a neighbor she and Brody had been feuding with for decades.

Lexi tried to unruffled her feathers. "Gram, he's his own worst enemy."

She shot back, "Not while I'm alive."

Lexi managed to get off the phone, but not before Doris accused her of giving her the "bum's rush."

Detective Reiger may have become a father figure and Julia a surrogate mother, but this was her real family, warts and all.

6

POKER NIGHT

The once-a-month poker game was usually at Ben's house in the Sunset District by the ocean. It was a few bus rides from her apartment on Russian Hill. It took the kind of time Lexi needed to plan. She threw a book and her Walkman into her bag. She patted Saxman, her old black-and-tan cat who did not like to be patted like a dog, and said goodbye.

It was dark and had started to rain again by the time she stood on Ben's stoop. She knocked and turned off the Walkman. The song, "Everybody Wants To Rule The World," died in her ears. Ben, the head baker at McCracken's, swung the door open as if he were fleeing the premises.

"Lexi!" He rushed at her with open arms. His hug nearly knocked her over.

"Welcome!" This intense friendliness was a change from when they had worked together. At the bakery, Ben terrified everyone with his exacting ways and quick temper. Now that he was home and more relaxed, they could tease him about how the Marines had made him obsessed with things being "squared away."

Inside, Lexi kicked her boots off and flung them on top of a neat pile of shoes near the door. It was warm and bright inside the old Victorian home. She followed Ben down a narrow hall that led to the living room at the back of the house. It smelled of garlic and fish broth. Furniture had been pushed to the walls to make room for the poker table.

Lexi said hello to Henry. He was wearing a well-made but worn suit, his hair slicked back and flattened from wearing a hat. She looked under the table. Henry was still wearing his dress shoes. Lexi thought how patient Minh, Ben's girlfriend, was with them. It would have embarrassed Henry to take off his shoes even though it was the house rule and a Vietnamese custom.

Stella croaked a "Hello." Her take-no-prisoners bangs extended well below her large glasses—as usual, she needed a trim. Her voice often gave out on her, but her demeanor made up for her failing voice.

Lexi sat next to Victor, the McCracken of McCracken's Bakery.

"Where's Timm?" asked Stella. "As our dearly departed friend Dean would say if he were here and alive, 'We're a cocktail short of a party without Timm.'"

Ben sat next to Minh. "It's hard for him to make it out this far from home. So I said next time we'll meet at his place." Timm was a dwarf and used crutches to walk. He lived near McCracken's, corner markets, bars and strip clubs in the Tenderloin—far from the beach.

They played a few hands. Lexi was playing badly and her mood darkened. She told Henry to chest his cards.

"What the hell is wrong with you?" Ben snapped.

She seemed to shrink. "I have something to tell you," she said quietly. Everyone looked up from the table and shifted in their seats.

"Remember I told you about my boss, David Emerson?"

Stella said, "Don't tell me they found him with an axe to the head?"

Lexi blushed. "Close."

Ben laughed so hard he started to cough. After catching his breath he said, "Lexi, you are the kiss of death!"

She wasn't hurt by his remark since Ben had helped to save her life. She understood better now that he had no filter since coming back from

Vietnam. She had even come to appreciate his bluntness.

A chorus of "When? "How?" and "Who did it?" came from her friends.

Henry said, "From what you've told us, it's a strange group at that place. Could one of them be the killer?"

"Why do you work there, again?" Stella interrupted.

Lexi said, "I was running from Jerry—his memory at least."

"And from us?" asked Ben.

"No." Lexi smiled. "Not from any of you."

"Are there any leads?" asked Henry.

"Not yet," Lexi answered. Henry looked concerned. "Take care of yourself."

"Watch your back, more like it." Ben picked up his cards. "You aren't in Kansas anymore or what did we used to say?"

"I heard you call her 'a country bumpkin' from Alaska," Henry said softly. "No one can call you that anymore." He reassured Lexi with a kind smile.

Stella punched Ben in the arm. She said, "Whose turn is it?" It was a tough crowd.

Minh gave Ben a reassuring squeeze with her free hand and set down a straight flush with the other. His pockmarked face melted into a toothy smile.

"That's my Nguyen-er," Ben beamed. He got a kick out of pronouncing her last name "win."

"It's a good thing the pot goes to your charity, Minh," said Stella. "Otherwise we'd resent how often you win."

Minh said, "It's really for Dean. The APLA needs the money. Otherwise, those poor men would have no dentist. It's shameful." Dean had been Ben's assistant at the bakery until he got sick.

Victor sighed. "Yeah, we know. Minh's the big win-her."

Lexi looked at Victor and Ben, friends since elementary school. At one time, she had suspected both of them of Jerry's murder. Looking at Victor now as his thick hair stood straight up making him look like a large Teddy Bear, she couldn't imagine he could hurt anyone. Ben was another story.

Minh giggled as she swept her arms across the table collecting any remaining chips. They started playing another hand when Ben looked at his watch. "We have plenty of money for Elizabeth Taylor and her AmFAR pals tonight. I have to get up at five. Out you lot go." He stood and everyone set their cards face up on the table. "Early to rise."

"Bastard!" Victor yelled. "I had a royal flush."

Ben smiled. "Get your royal flush ass out of my house."

It was midnight when Lexi opened the door to her apartment. Saxman was asleep on the futon. Her hearing was going and she did not wake. Lexi turned on the wall heater and stripped in front of the furnace, letting the heat wash over her.

She picked up her pajamas crumpled next to the futon and put them on. She curled herself around Saxman, who started to purr, and threw the comforter over them both.

7

MRS. JACKIE REIGER

Detective Robert Reiger sat at his kitchen table and watched Jackie clean the dinner dishes. When he came home from work, the first thing he did was hang up his leather jacket, smoothing the shoulders before hanging it in the entryway closet.

Though slightly rundown, this part of Oakland had the look of any-town America with tree-lined streets of Craftsman and colonial houses. The Reiger home was a small bungalow built in the early 1900s with Palladian windows and a large porch. There were gray shingles upstairs and white clapboard siding on the bottom floor. The house had been in Reiger's family since his father had moved from the south to work as a longshoreman at the Oakland docks during the Second Great Migration during WWII.

Outside, the leaves on the maple trees had recently turned rust-red and buttery yellow. The dim streetlights filtered through the trees casting ghostly shadows.

Inside, the kitchen was warm. The smell of pasta and greens lingered. Reiger stood at the sink, filling the kettle with water. Jackie leaned against the kitchen table, drying her hands as she watched her husband.

"Why are you giving that white girl the time of day?" she asked, unable to hold back. "Shouldn't she be a suspect?" Jackie could be quick to anger, but she could also let it go just as fast. Reiger looked at his wife, smiled and shook his head. "I knew there was something on your mind."

They had met in college and hadn't been apart for more than a few days since. Jackie moved closer, leaning into Robert as his arms drew her in.

"Jackie, I don't tell you how to teach your third graders." He moved her head gently so he could look into her dark eyes. "What is this about?"

"She's not like Jada." Robert gave his wife a look of such love that she began to cry. Their daughter had been gone for six years. The loss was unbearable but they had agreed that they would not bury themselves along with their beloved Jada. Some couples could not live with that kind of grief and each other, but Robert and Jackie had clung to one another as if in a lifeboat on an angry sea.

The kettle whistled, but they let it wail.

8

FRIDAY, OCTOBER 18, 1985—
AN UNLIKELY REUNION

The next morning in North Beach, Lexi grabbed a cappuccino to go before catching the bus. She hid the cup from the driver and tried not to spill it inside her book-bag as the bus drove down Columbus Avenue, jockeying for space with cars. Detective Reiger had asked her to come in early to beat the other staff members to work.

It was another foggy morning but not as wet as the day before. Reiger was sitting at Lexi's desk going over his notes when she came in.

"Morning," he said, standing and moving aside. Something was different about him. The raincoat was gone, replaced by the leather jacket she had noticed the day before.

"You're a leather jacket guy now?" she asked.

"People change," he said, not unkindly. "How have you been?"

Lexi threw her bag under the desk and sat down. She smiled weakly. "You are so nice to ask. I'm okay. Since Jerry died, I've been trying to move past him so that I can have a relationship."

"You have a boyfriend?"

"Yeah, Cosmo. He drives an ambulance, but he's studying to be a paramedic."

"Another rescuer."

"I know. I hear it all the time from Ben and my bakery friends. What is wrong with me? Jerry was a fireman and now I'm with an EMT."

"There's nothing wrong with you. I'm teasing. As long as he's good to you."

"He is. He knows I'm the girl from the newspapers, but I can't talk about what happened to Jerry when he brings it up."

Reiger's eyes seemed to soften. He said, "You know, you remind me of my daughter."

"You have a daughter?"

"Had a daughter. She was taken from us in a hit-and-run in '79."

They were silent for a while. Lexi avoided looking at his face to give him time to regain his composure. "How old was she?"

"15."

"She'd be 21, my age." Lexi was tearing up, but forced herself to stop. Before yesterday, it had been two years since she had talked with Reiger. She was relieved that what she considered to be a friendship had continued. She didn't want to burden him with her sadness. "What was she like?"

"Curious, kind, smart." Reiger looked embarrassed. "I'm not sure why I told you that. My wife, Jackie, was upset with me because she thinks I'm not treating you like a suspect."

Lexi rested her hand on her cheek. "I don't know that treating someone like a suspect would help you catch a guilty person. You might pretend to be friendly to trip somebody up, right? You'd always catch your killer."

Reiger smiled, thinking that Lexi was curious, kind and smart. He shifted a book from the bookshelf. "Let's get to it, shall we?"

"Sure."

He sat. "I've asked the employees we didn't talk to yesterday to come in for interviews today. Before they get here, tell me more about David."

"He was good at his job," Lexi said.

"Did anyone hate him enough to kill him?"

"I can't imagine it. Jack was right. David was all about the money. I'm not sure that would get him killed. It feels very libertarian."

"It's not a warm and fuzzy philosophy."

"Not so much."

They heard the door open as Peggy walked in. Threads hung from the bottom of her unbuttoned overcoat. She wore a rumpled Tahari suit. Her hair had not seen a comb in some time. "Oh!" She started when she saw Reiger as if she had forgotten that it was not just another day.

He introduced himself, and Peggy stood awkwardly at the desk holding a soggy paper bag with what Lexi guessed was lunch. An enormous and full Hermès purse that had seen better days hung open, slipping off Peggy's shoulder. She was juggling a stack of books in the crook of her arm.

Reiger thought better of extending his hand for a shake. "We talked on the phone yesterday. Detective Reiger. Please sit."

They sat down, Peggy's armful spilled around her. Reiger opened his notebook.

"Peggy, what is your position here?"

She stammered, "I'm—I'm—am I in trouble?"

"Not yet." Reiger gave her a reassuring smile.

Her shoulders relaxed. "I'm an editor and a writer. Every book needs a thorough proposal that gets approved by the donor funding the book." She leaned closer to Reiger and said, "Just between us and the fern," she motioned to the potted plant in the corner, "I write most of the books. Ghostwrite them."

Lexi was in disbelief. She started to wonder if she knew anything about what when on at The Freedom Institute or the people she worked with.

Reiger asked Peggy, "And what was your relationship with David?"

"I liked him fine. He wasn't very nice but I don't need nice as long as the paychecks don't bounce. David was very good at raising money."

"Tell me how it works. How does the money flow?"

"I don't know. You'll have to ask Julia."

Lexi reminded him, "Office manager." She remembered that Reiger was familiar with Peggy's husband, but wasn't sure if he wanted Peggy to know that. "Peggy's husband, Grey, takes pictures at our events."

Reiger looked from Lexi to Peggy. "Does he?"

"Oh, oh, yeah. David throws him some work. Grey's an antique book dealer. He's an authenticator too," she said proudly. "But it's hard for him to let go of the most valuable books, if you know what I mean."

"A man of many talents. Did your husband acquire books for David?"

"No." Peggy shook her head, sending drops of water over the pile splayed around her. "No. No. Grey would never do that. David was only extravagant with other people's money. He could be downright cheap."

Reiger didn't want to bring up the *Atlas Shrugged* in David's office until he knew for sure where it had come from.

"Did this cheapness extend to the Institute? Did he meet payroll?"

"Yes! Libertarians have deep pockets. We have a working budget, I think. Julia would know. We mostly always got our paychecks." Reiger raised an eyebrow. She continued, "I mean we always get them, but sometimes they're a day late. I always insisted he pays Grey before a gig."

"I'll need to speak to your husband." He closed his notebook. "Whom do you think would harm David?"

Peggy laughed. "Take your pick."

"Why are you laughing?" Detective Reiger had seen this reaction many times. It was a nervous response that could be innocent, but he could sense there was something else.

Peggy shifted on the couch, her damp overcoat squeaking on the leather. "I can tell you that David had enemies, but nobody *here* wanted him dead."

Reiger waited.

"I'd look at his wife. They have twins, babies. It's them I feel sorry for. Let's just say that David would go to great lengths to secure a donation."

"Mrs. Neville, this is no time to be coy. Are you saying David was stealing money?"

"Oh, no, he wouldn't be that vulgar. At least I don't think he would." Peggy's eyes drifted to the bookshelf, lost in thought. Reiger cleared his throat, and her focus returned. "I'm saying look at Renée."

"Renée?" Lexi asked with a laugh.

Peggy looked triumphant. "I think she's secretly in love with him." Having dropped the bombshell, the interview quickly came to a close. Peggy left the reception area and went to her office.

Lexi remembered an argument she had witnessed between Peggy and David in his office a few days before, and told Reiger. Peggy had tried to drum up work for Grey and accused David of having no black employees.

Peggy had pleaded with him, "Don't you see the blinding whiteness of this office?"

David was silent, indignant.

"There isn't one minority working here."

"So what?" David had said. "If there were qualified candidates, I would have hired them."

Peggy sounded furious. "Don't give me that libertarian crap!"

"I hire Grey, don't I? What's gotten into you?"

Lexi heard him say, "I have a meeting" before he had walked into the reception area. He turned to Peggy and said, "Get yourself together by the time I get back."

Once he was gone, a stunned Lexi had asked Peggy if she was okay. She had slumped on the couch and admitted that Grey had lost a big book deal, a first edition of a Ralph Ellison. It had been a great price, and he could have sold it to a private dealer for a small fortune.

Lexi remembered the conversation because she had written "Ralph Ellison" on a piece of paper. She wanted to look him up during her next library visit. Because she hadn't gone to college, she had a lot of catching up to do.

Reiger said, "Tell me anything else that you can remember about that exchange."

Lexi recounted that Peggy told her she and Grey had a house full of priceless books but no money. She was sorry she had made the case to David about how white this place was.

"How did the conversation end?" asked Reiger.

"It was nothing to do with David. Peggy said she thought of Alaska as the whitest place in America before I reminded her about Native Americans like the Tlingit and Haida tribes. I thought she was going to be mad, but she laughed and said to forgive her, and that David brought out the worst in her."

They were interrupted by a knock at the door. A tall dark man in a blue FedEx uniform with an envelope tucked under his arm came into the room.

"Hi, Walter," Lexi said, as if her dead boss hadn't been moved from his office to the morgue the day before.

Walter handed Lexi an envelope and turned the metal clipboard around for her to sign.

She looked at Reiger, who nodded.

She signed the form and Walter nodded respectfully to Detective Reiger before disappearing as fast as he had appeared, just as Jack seemed to materialize from nowhere.

"When did you get here?" Detective Reiger asked.

"Been here for ages, old—" Jack eyed the package on Lexi's desk "—man."

Ignoring Jack, Reiger stroked his graying mustache and said, "I'll need a better place for interviews."

"The conference room," said Lexi. "Down the hall to the right."

"What about me?" Jack whined. "I have work to do. Is that for me?" He eyed the package again.

"Of course it is." Lexi looked at Reiger before handing Jack the envelope stuffed with packets of cocaine.

9

MULTIPLYING SUSPECTS

Reiger was interviewing Jack in Jack's own office. The detective recognized the well-cut suit as one he had seen in the window of Wilkes Bashford, made famous by its most well-known customer, California's Assembly Speaker Willie Brown.

"Tell me about Julia."

"Julia! Don't be fooled by those polished nails and Ann Taylor dresses. She's a lush. She knows everything that goes on here, front of house and back. But she's harmless." Jack was talking fast. "You know, I have to admit that she's good at HR. So, who cares if she has a little wine at lunch," he paused for maximum effect. "Or a bottle or two."

Reiger watched Jack pacing the floor. He could see that Jack was exaggerating to shield his own bad behavior. "What about the Institute's finances?"

"Ah! Now that's the question, old man." Reiger raised his eyebrow, but Jack wasn't paying attention. "David would snatch a dime out of a dead man's hand. He was the fundraising king."

Leaning back in the chair, Reiger changed it up. "How about Ms. Fagan?"

Jack laughed. "Ms.! You know she's from Alaska! I ask you: Who's from Alaska?" He paused for a nanosecond. "She's a good kid. Terrible speller."

"What was her relationship with David?"

"She was afraid of him. He was a bully. A real cretin, but I got along with him."

Reiger said, "A cretin is a stupid person. Was David stupid?"

"No," Jack stuttered. "Yes, I mean he was a bright guy, but he couldn't keep his pants on, if you know what I mean. Not that there's anything wrong with that, but I'm not married, if you know what I mean."

Jack had a high opinion of himself. Reiger asked, "Do you have a gut feeling about who might have wanted to kill David?"

"Like I said before, follow the money. David skimmed off the top."

"Are you saying he embezzled from his own company?"

Jack paused. Reiger followed Jack's eyes as they darted around the room before resting on the steel crossbeams in front of the window. Still staring, Jack said, "Let's say he moved the money around."

Reiger wanted to wrap it up. "What about David's wife?"

"Mrs. Amy Davenport Emerson! She knew what she was marrying. But it was a big blow when she found out about Mary."

"Mary?"

"Our biggest donor besides the Clark brothers. The granddaughter of Francis Fairchild, Fairchild Grocery." He looked at Reiger as if thought he was born yesterday. "David and Mary. Going at it." Jack made a vulgar gesture. He sat down and fidgeted in his chair.

Reiger remembered David's calendar. That Mary. He stood and walked to the door.

"It seems you have an expensive lifestyle. I know how much you're paid. How can you afford it?" Reiger was bluffing about the salary, but he knew no amount of money could keep up with a serious coke habit.

Jack leaned back in his chair, spreading his legs, pretending to relax. "I have rich parents. It's called 'libertarian privilege.' Unless you come from a communist country and hate everything collective like Ayn Rand did, having money helps the libertarian cause."

Reiger nodded. "Thank you for your time. I spoke with your date. Your alibi checks out."

Jack snorted. Before leaving, Reiger turned and said, "And cocaine is illegal, Mr. Abbott. If you don't stop having it shipped to you, I will have you arrested and charged."

Reiger rounded the corner. Lexi was sitting at the reception desk. "Peggy?" he asked. Lexi pointed to an office to the right. "Don't go anywhere," he said before he knocked on Peggy's door. "I need to talk to you."

"Come in!" Peggy opened the door as if she had been waiting nervously on the other side. Reiger stepped in to the small book-lined office. He noticed many of the books were not on libertarianism, but were fiction. Some of them looked as if they might be from her husband's collection. Peggy sat down. She picked up the cigarette burning in an ashtray on her desk.

"Excuse me, Detective, I want to do something before I forget."

Reiger nodded his assent. He took a book from the shelf and flipped it open while he waited.

Peggy picked up the receiver and buzzed Lexi. "What were those tribe names again? There's a libertarian angle on the Indians. I'm thinking a book on sovereignty."

After writing a note, she hung up and motioned for Reiger to sit.

"Do you keep many first editions at work?"

Peggy giggled. "I'm hiding that from my husband."

Reiger said, "Grey Neville."

"Yeah." She looked puzzled. "Do you know him?"

"I know of him. There aren't many black antique book dealers in the East Bay."

"Not many black detectives in San Francisco, either, I'd guess." She smiled and motioned for him to sit in a plush armchair that took up most of the space in front of Peggy's desk. Reiger replaced the book and sank into the chair.

"Are you a book hound, too?" she asked.

"Not a collector, just a reader. Tell me about Grey taking photographs at Freedom Institute events."

"Oh, yes! As I told you, Grey has a hard time selling his treasures, so David throws him some work."

"Has there been conflict between them? Anything unpleasant?"

"No. Nothing like that." Peggy scoffed. "Grey likes David. Besides, we have a lot of fundraisers and book launches. It keeps us afloat."

"So, you write book proposals and ghostwrite the books?"

"Yes."

Reiger noticed that Peggy was quite pretty. She had a broad smile and intelligent green eyes. Reiger guessed she was in her early 40s. Though white people sometimes looked older than their years would suggest. The smoking didn't help.

"Is ghostwriting common at think tanks?"

"Not really. People like to write their own books, but David is—was—very persuasive. Despite what he thought, our books actually sell pretty well because they aren't as academic as most. And I'm a good writer. You know, there are authors he promised big contracts and big paychecks to that never materialized. There's another motivated group."

Reiger liked Peggy. "You mean after his wife, his lover, his employees, his former employer— and what was Juanita's motive?"

"Very funny. She's probably the only person who didn't care one way or another if David existed."

The door opened and Renée stuck her head in. Seeing Detective Reiger, she stopped short.

"What is it?" Peggy asked.

"I was looking for the negatives from the fundraiser for the last newsletter."

"Why would I have those?"

"Because your husband was the photographer."

Peggy laughed. "Oh, hon. Jack has 'em. Mr. Director is writing the copy."

Without replying, Renée closed the door. Reiger gave Peggy a quizzical look. "We're always behind. Our last fundraiser was in the spring but we haven't managed to get the newsletter out. But, I guarantee it will happen. We'll keep going, even now when we're like chickens with our heads cut off without David."

Peggy looked toward the door where Renée had been standing. "I recommended her for the job, but she can get on my nerves. She's in everyone's business."

Reiger said, "Renée's husband has a lot of clout. Was there tension between him and David?"

"No." They liked each other. "David was Ralph's kind of guy. When David struck out on his own, it make Ralph respect him even more." Peggy took a long drag on her cigarette. "There is something odd about that couple. For some reason, Ralph doesn't come to many of our events. He always seems to be out of town." Peggy paused. "I know it grates on Renée, but she would never say anything against him."

"How did Renée feel about David?"

"She was like a moth to a flame." Peggy stubbed out her cigarette. "The Institute is like having her own private think tank."

"She had no reason to hurt him?"

"I was letting my imagination get the best of me," she said, distracted. "No."

Reiger lifted the book he was holding. He read, "Twenty Love Poems and a Song of Despair."

"Neruda. My favorite."

"You were saying—" Reiger tried to get back on track. "About the writers."

"Of course." Peggy's attention snapped back. "Writers are often promised contracts that don't come through."

"Do you have someone in mind?"

"They're policy wonks and nerds. I don't think these guys have much passion for anything but ideas."

"How does he get authors to agree? He must have a terrible reputation."

"They're not best-selling authors to begin with. You know, academics have to write books but they don't have to be good ones. David convinced them their books would sell, and he pays well once the book is done and in the catalogue. Everyone has an ego. It's actually very libertarian of David. It's what I admired about him. He walked the walk." Peggy reached for a pack of cigarettes and nodded to Reiger for permission to light up again. He shook his head in affirmation. Putting potential suspects at ease was the name of the game.

Peggy lit the Pall Mall. She blew the smoke away from Detective Reiger before continuing. "Most of the employees here don't care about the ideals. I find it disheartening. There are a lot of places you can work, so why work here?"

"Why then?"

"That was a rhetorical question. We have Clark brothers' money."

Reiger said, "They also fund the Reed Foundation." Peggy cocked her head, impressed with Reiger's knowledge of libertarian politics. "Why fund two libertarian organizations?" Reiger stood. The smoke burned his eyes. "Can I open this window?"

"Be my guest." Peggy rested the cigarette in an overflowing ashtray. Reiger stood and cracked the window.

"The Clarks like to keep everyone on their toes. Competition is the name of the libertarian game, so they spread their money around and make sure everyone knows it. They're very rich and very powerful. There's a lot of pressure to put out more books than Reed. Ralph also likes to keep Renée busy. Having her here keeps us busy."

Reiger took a deep breath of damp air before sitting down. "How long have you been here?"

"Oh, yonks. I've written over 70 books and hundreds of proposals."

"Mrs. Neville, how did you feel about David?"

"Mixed. He brought me over from Reed and I was flattered until I realized he wanted me to write 90 percent of the books. It's been a big job, but I'm grateful to him. I didn't like him, but I wouldn't want to see him harmed. He's got a family."

"Who do you think had a grudge against him besides his wife because of the affair?" Reiger took another deep breath before Peggy lit another cigarette. The first one still smoldered in the ashtray. She took a drag before answering. "It's not like David was a great guy, but he kept this place running and all of us employed. But, to be honest, there were a few that held grudges."

"Could you be more specific?"

"Okay." Peggy was more into dishing dirt than Reiger would have expected from a true believer.

"Jack's habit." She tapped the side of her nose. "David promised him a raise so he wouldn't take a job at Reed. David left Reed to start this place. It would have killed him to lose anyone to them. But from what I gather, David never came through with the money."

"That seemed to be a pattern." Reiger made a note. "Anything else about Renée?"

"She's always on me about finishing the books faster, but she has a tough job. She keeps the authors away from me, so I don't care if she's a pain."

"Why have a Renée at all?" asked Reiger. "Can't David talk with the authors about their books? Or you?"

Peggy let out a full belly laugh. "David doesn't read our books! He's a salesman. Thank whatever mutation created the Renées of the world. I have too much on my plate to deal with fragile male egos." She went back to an earlier thought. "Ask Julia if David had done something to hurt Renée or make her mad. They're pretty tight."

Reiger had gotten what he came for. It was getting close to lunch and he still needed to follow up with Lexi.

10

LATER THAT DAY

Reiger walked into the reception area and leaned against the wall. He said with a casual tone, "You haven't been honest with me."

Lexi wasn't sure where this was going, so she waited.

He said, "Jack."

"Oh, Jack!" She was relieved. "I thought you were going to say Julia."

"Tell me about both and make it quick." He glanced at his watch. "It's getting late."

Lexi opened her desk drawer, pulled out an apple and offered it to Reiger.

"No, thanks."

"Well, I don't blame you. Someone was poisoned here recently."

"How do you know that?" Reiger's tone was no longer casual.

"Juanita." Lexi put the apple away.

"Doesn't she work nights?" Reiger asked.

"She does but when we have a conference here or a weekend board meeting, she comes in to serve sandwiches and coffee. We're friends. One time, she told me that she saw a poisoning when she was a kid. It's not the kind of thing you forget. She saw David's face and the vomit. She was just guessing. Sorry if I sprang that on you. She didn't want to be here by herself at night so Julia changed her shift to days. She'll serve coffee at meetings and—"

"Lexi."

"Right. She just told me about the poison this morning."

"Why didn't Juanita tell us that?"

"She loves fictional detectives but is actually afraid of the police."

Reiger pulled a chair near the desk and sat down. "I want you to tell me everything."

Lexi told him that Jack had a coke habit and that Julia did drink some during the day but that it didn't impair her work and that she was a loyal and wonderful boss and friend.

"Okay. I get it. You're grateful to Julia, but not so loyal to Jack."

"He expects me to cover for his deliveries. Libertarians believe drugs should be legal."

When Reiger didn't respond Lexi said, "What are you going to do about the coke?"

"Libertarians may wish that drugs were legal, but they're not. I told Jack to put a stop to it and you will tell me if he receives any more packages. You have my permission to open anything he gets if you think it's suspicious. I need you to work with me here, Lexi."

She nodded with what she hoped was as serious an expression as she felt. She hated the idea of disappointing him.

Reiger continued. "Jack has expensive taste. When I asked him about it, he said that his family is wealthy. Ask around."

Lexi couldn't help but grin and quickly agreed. Before Reiger left, Lexi told him they were closing the office early to get ready for the fundraiser.

11

POST MORTEM

After lunch, Reiger met Dr. Yu at the morgue in the basement of San Francisco General Hospital. Morgues were always cold and Detective Reiger was glad he had dressed for the Arctic. His leather jacket fit snug over a heavy sweater. He was staring at Dr. Yu's lab coat. The patch with the Medical Examiner symbol was tie-dyed purple and orange.

Dr. Yu shrugged. "My students. They think they're funny."

"I'd say they are funny." Reiger noticed Yu eyeing his leather jacket. "No. You don't need to say anything about my fly jacket now."

Yu gave him an innocent look. Reiger walked to the stainless steel table where David Emerson's body was covered with a sheet.

"What do you have to tell me?"

"Oh, this is a good one." Yu pulled the sheet down to the body's waist. "We were right. He's been poisoned, but it was only enough to make him sick." Yu moved David's head to the side, exposing a deep wound at the back. "The gash to his skull is what killed him."

"Time of death?"

"I'd say between 10:00 and midnight."

Dr. Yu looked at the body, sewn in a rough zig-zag from the pubic area to the chest, split across the collarbone to each shoulder in a gruesome "Y."

Reiger observed, "What's with the Dr. Frankenstein stitches? You're usually so meticulous."

Yu shrugged. "Students. They don't have the skill or the respect for the dead yet." He paused. "They haven't learned that the body always tells a story. It's a story of a life and of a death. They don't know how to listen for the story yet."

Reiger wanted to tease Yu about his philosophizing, but he respected his colleague and friend. Besides, it was a nice sentiment though he couldn't let it lie. "I'm going to lift that for my report."

Yu grinned.

"Have you tested the contents of David's stomach?"

"Is that your euphemistic way of asking about the vomit? Of course. Mushrooms. The poison of witches."

"Fool's mushroom?" asked Reiger.

Yu laughed. "Now you're just showing off! No. Destroying angels."

They looked at the body for a moment in silence before Reiger said, "That wound on the head. Whadya figure?"

"Something handy. This looks frenzied to me. Maybe the poisoner realized it wasn't working or not working fast enough, and they attacked him?"

"I thought of that." Reiger pulled the picture of David sitting at his desk from his pocket. Yu scanned the image. On the desk were framed pictures, a paperweight, a few books and a five-inch-tall glass pyramid shaped like the Transamerica building. Reiger pointed to the statue. "Know what this is?" Yu shook his head, "No."

"It's a Trannie." Yu laughed. Reiger continued, "It's the Transamerica Award. The Chamber of Commerce gives it to businesses that threaten to leave San Francisco, but decide to stay despite the high taxes. It's like a game."

"Hoisted with his own petard," said Yu. When Reiger didn't respond to his joke, Yu said, "You know. Killed with an award. Poetic justice."

"Not your best work, Yu." He took the picture and returned it to his pocket. "The Trannie wasn't there yesterday."

"Congratulations, David Emerson," said Yu, covering the body with a sheet. "You won that game."

At the office, Lexi asked Peggy if Jack were rich.

"No way. He's all flash and no pan. I don't know how he can afford to party at Club Nine every night. He takes cabs everywhere—and those suits! Personally I don't care what he does, but things have never added up with that guy."

As soon as Detective Reiger had left, the staff took off in order to prepare for the fundraiser. Lexi hung back to poke around Jack's office. Maybe there were clues to how Jack afforded his lifestyle. She had no idea how that might lead to David's killer, but she almost couldn't help herself from snooping. Normally, employees locked their doors at night. To her surprise, Jack's door was unlocked. There had been nothing normal since she had arrived at the office the morning before.

She left the lights off. It felt more clandestine somehow; besides, there was light coming through the window. A wing-back chair was next to a small side table with the Institute's newsletters stacked on top. At the window, there were steel beams like the ones in most downtown office windows to protect against earthquakes. It gave the room a hip, edgy vibc.

A small couch with a plexiglass coffee table sat in front of the steel "X." The walls were exposed brick. Lexi moved a stack of magazines near the edge of the coffee table and noticed scratch marks on the surface. Razor blade cuts. On a hunch, she got up and ran her hand along the back of the steel beams. There it was. A packet of powder jammed under the lip. She put it back and continued her search.

The desk drawers were locked. She took a letter opener and slid it along the top of the left drawer like she had seen in a movie. The lock clicked open. Pleased, she opened the drawer and gently lifted out envelopes and papers. One of the envelopes was from The Reed Foundation. It contained a check stub for $100,000. She put everything back as she had found it and opened the middle drawer using her super-sleuth technique. She couldn't wait to tell Cosmo how easy it had been.

There was nothing in the drawer but a yellow legal pad. The pages were blank, but there were deep indentations on the top page. She took a pencil and gently rubbed across the surface.

It read, "donation = $300,000 Mary" and "DE going for Reed biggest donor dog."

She gently tore out the page, folded it and put it in her jacket pocket. This is easy, she thought just as the door flew open.

Jack walked in and put on the light. "What the hell are you doing in here?"

Lexi got up and walked to the front of the desk. "I was looking for the latest newsletter. I'm so sorry." She had to think fast. Words tumbled out of her. "Your door was open and I found this on your desk." She grabbed a mock-up of the upcoming newsletter. "Julia asked for the book list. Do you mind if I make a copy? I promise to return it." It was a plausible excuse, and Jack relaxed a little. "I guess. Go ahead." He looked at the steel beams. "I forgot something." He waited for Lexi to leave the office, which she did right away. She knew he was retrieving his weekend supply.

When Jack left it was 1:00 p.m. Lexi decided to go to the library before the fundraiser. She wanted to look up libertarianism and pick up a book by Ralph Ellison. When she applied for the job, she had not been curious about what kind of place it was. She wanted the opposite of the bakery, to put space between her and Jerry's memory. Now she wished she had known more.

Before leaving the office, she stopped at the bathroom and put a roll of toilet paper in her book-bag to use on the houseboat. No more cheap TP for her.

12

THE LIBRARY

The fog had burned away, and it was a bright cool day. Lexi walked down to Market Street and took a bus to Van Ness Avenue. City Hall and the SF Public Library were a few blocks away. The short walk from the bus felt good. The wind was cold, but her vintage men's suit jacket and turtleneck kept her warm.

Once in the library, she browsed the fiction aisles looking for "E" authors when she felt someone close behind her. She turned quickly. Wicked Smith was grinning at her.

"You scared the daylights out of me!" Lexi was angry.

"What's that?" he said. "An Alaska saying? Since it's daylight all night?"

Wicked worked in the stock room at the Institute packing and shipping books. He never let anyone in the mysterious stock room. His other duties were to make sure galleys of the books were delivered to authors for review. He mailed newsletters and took care of everything mail-related.

Looking back, she could not believe that she had dated him shortly after joining The Freedom Institute. On their one and only night out, she had noticed his strange gait and asked him why he walked with a limp. He had told her that his foot had been cut off jumping a train in Oakland on his way to watch Evel Knievel jump a motorcycle over a dozen cars. She thought he was joking and had laughed until he pulled his pant leg up, exposing a plastic prosthetic leg. He had been good-humored about her faux pas. Luckily, he had not liked her any more than she did him, so there was no need to beg off of a second date.

Wicked put his arm on the bookshelf and leaned close to Lexi. His leather jacket was full of buckles, but none of them were in use, exposing a V-neck t-shirt over stiff jeans.

The last place she expected to see Wicked was at a library.

"Penny?" Wicked said. He had a habit of truncating phrases and words like "uni" for "university" and "penny" for "penny for your thoughts" which Lexi, once she realized what he was trying to say, found annoying.

"What are you doing here?" she asked.

"What? Because I'm a musician I'm not allowed at the library?" Lexi saw the records in the crook of his free arm. "The Sex Pistols, huh?"

"That's right." Wicked did have a winning smile and his hair fell into his eyes in a not unpleasant way. "I can't afford Tower Records. Why pay when I can check out records for free here."

Lexi pictured a way for Wicked to make extra cash and made a mental note to stop any schemes where he would sign for Jack's special deliveries.

"You haven't been in the office. You heard about David?"

"Yeah, man, what a bummer." He seemed genuinely upset. "I got a call from a detective to stay home 'til Monday."

"How come you never had a beef with David?" Lexi was in full detective mode.

"He left me alone." Wicked shook his head. "I liked him. Even if I know things about him that would make your skin crawl."

"Like what?"

"That's for me to know."

"Oh for crying out loud," Lexi said.

"For what?!" Wicked choked with laughter as Lexi crossed her arms defensively.

There was that grin again. "Keep your shirt on. David's a dog. I mean, he was a dog."

Lexi didn't want to let on that she knew about David's affair. She wanted to tread lightly. She had convinced herself that when she could prove that Julia was not a suspect she would stay out of the rest of the investigation. If she pushed it too far, she would lose the trust of Detective Reiger, maybe for good.

She might get more out of Wicked if she played dumb. "David? Really?"

He set his records on the table and sat down. He leaned back in the chair like a bad school kid and motioned for Lexi to take a seat. She sat and moved the chair closer.

"Okay. David the dog was sleeping with our biggest donor," he paused, looked around and leaned in for full effect. "Mary Fairchild."

Lexi feigned surprise. "No!" But then a question she hadn't thought of before came to mind. "Why would anyone but Mrs. Emerson care about that?"

"Oh, my naive friend. That's only the tip of the iceberg."

Lexi leaned back so as not to seem too eager.

"Gretchen Stenholm." Wicked clapped his hands in triumph. They both quickly looked around to see if he had attracted attention. They seemed to be in a deserted corner.

"Our Gretchen?" Lexi was confused. "You mean David was sleeping with her too? Well, that means his wife and Mary each had a motive."

"Or Gretchen maybe wanted him to herself. I'm not sayin' —" Wicked was pleased with himself. "I'm just sayin', mate."

"Wicked, have you ever set foot in England?"

"Nah. But everyone got to have an angle, right?" He looked at the clock on the wall. It was just after 4:00 p.m. "Hey, I gotta scoot. Got a gig tonight. Nap time." He stood and grabbed the records. "You should come. It's at the Sound of Music bar on Turk. Bring that boyfriend of yours, Cosmic wonder boy.

"Cosmo."

"Whatever. Who names their kid Cosmo?

Lexi stared at him. "Hello! Pot. Kettle."

A smile spread over Wicked's lips. "Good one. Bring your sci-fi boy toy."

"I can't. They haven't cancelled the fundraiser," Lexi reminded him.

Wicked laughed. "Isn't that the good 'ol libertines for ya! Never miss an opportunity to make money. It's been nice chattin'." He winked and walked away.

"See you Monday," called Lexi.

"Unless you have your eyes closed," He said over his shoulder as he disappeared behind a bookshelf.

She waved absently, deep in thought. Once, when Gretchen's office door had been ajar, Lexi had heard her on the phone with David's wife,

Amy. They seemed to be close friends. If Amy found out Gretchen and David were having an affair, would she have killed David? Would Gretchen be next? Lexi needed to find a pay phone to call Detective Reiger.

"That's what Wicked told me." Lexi was standing at a phone booth at the corner of Van Ness and Hayes talking to Reiger. "And Jack did not come from money. What he was doing was selling the Reed Institute information on our donors. I found a check stub for $100,000 in his desk." Before Reiger could ask how she had discovered it, she said, "Maybe David found out and Jack killed him? So that's Jack, Mary, Amy and possibly Gretchen with motives."

Reiger started talking as if Lexi were a stranger calling in a tip. "Well, I appreciate the information, ma'am."

"Is there someone in your office?"

"That's right, ma'am. Thank you for calling." The line went dead.

13

SERGEANT STRYKER

Detective Sergeant Emanuel Stryker was leaning on a filing cabinet, waiting. Reiger hung up the phone and looked at his boss. He had been two-finger typing his notes before the call when Stryker had walked in without knocking.

Stryker said, "I haven't been filled in on the Emerson case. The media is breathing down my neck."

That was Stryker's excuse for expecting updates every day when Reiger was working a case. It was not standard practice. Reiger was not just the only black detective in San Francisco; he was one of the few blacks on the force and had been promoted before Stryker took over the division. The Sergeant was the kind of leader who surrounded himself with loyalists who all happened to be white. Reiger had heard rumors that Stryker wasn't sure what to do with him. He wished he could say, "*Leave me to do my job,*" to Stryker's face.

Reiger's steady gaze met Stryker's as he told him about David's body, the time of death, and details from the medical examiner's report.

"Who's the examiner? The Chinaman?"

"You mean Dr. Yu." Reiger kept his tone neutral. "Dr. Yu's report was sent to you directly after the examination which occurred 24 hours after the body was moved to the morgue."

Unable to make hay, Stryker said, "By the book. Good. That's regulation. Good. Good."

In 1979, Detective Reiger had been given a high-profile murder case. He had expected to have the full resources of the department, but they never materialized. Dr. Yu had broken every rule in the book to get the forensics right, but it was not enough. The case was never solved. Reiger knew better, now. He would solve the case single-handedly if he had to. At least he had someone on the inside of the Institute, Lexi Fagan.

Reiger continued, "I have interviewed most of the staff at The Freedom Institute and will continue to do so. Emerson's wife has been notified and I will interview her shortly. Tonight is a fundraiser which the good libertarians feel free to go ahead with, even without their boss."

This seemed to spark Stryker's interest. "Anyone there I should know?"

"I couldn't say. It is a who's who of San Francisco society that will be mingling with suspects."

"Maybe I should attend?" Stryker said.

"I've got this, sir."

"Right. No overtime for this case unless the press hounds me even more."

Reiger suppressed a smile. The telephone numbers of the hounding press Stryker was whining about were programmed into the phone on Stryker's desk. It was more likely Stryker would be calling them to gin up publicity rather than the other way around.

Stryker looked at his watch. He signed heavily. "It's getting late. It's Friday. I have paperwork so I'll leave you to it." He walked to the door. "You'd better wrap it up yourself."

Reiger returned to typing his notes. "No overtime," he said.

14

FRIDAY, OCTOBER 18,

1985—HOME AGAIN

At home after the library, Lexi fed Saxman and flopped onto the futon. The apartment looked as if the Limited Express had exploded next to a Chinese takeout. She was not going to a punk rock club in the Tenderloin when she could have Ghirardelli hot chocolate made with real milk, and Saxman rubbing around her ankles, ready for her supper. There barely enough time for each activity before she had to change for the fundraiser.

Warm from the hot chocolate, she let her mind drift to thoughts of Jerry and their night at Manka's restaurant. That image was replaced by one of Cosmo dressed in his uniform. His handsome face smiling, his hair pulled into a loose ponytail. There was a part of her that would rather be home cuddled with Saxman or at Tower Records looking through tapes. On the other hand, Cosmo was a wonderful guy and always thought of fun things to do. Roller-skating. Dancing. *What's wrong with me?* she thought.

Time was running out. She got up and straightened the room. She glanced at the newspaper before throwing it in the trash. She saw the name Mary Fairchild in Herb Caen's column. She spread the paper on the table and read. Mary had attended the opening of a winery in Sonoma the night David had been murdered. She could have arranged to meet him at the office later, Lexi thought. She read on. The gossip in the column was that Mary had stayed overnight with a young man from the grocery lobby. Maybe things had cooled with David?

Once Detective Reiger stepped inside his home, tension drained from his body. He took off his leather jacket and hung it carefully in the closet, walked into the kitchen and sat down heavily at the table. His wife was sewing a button on one of his work shirts. Reiger hoped the topic of Lexi Fagan would not come up.

"How was your day?" she asked, not taking her eyes from her work.

"Oh, no. You first." She looked up and smiled. Jackie was a third-grade teacher at Franklin Elementary. She described her students to him as "open-hearted and sweet." Halloween was around the corner and that made everyone happy. Except for the year Jada had been killed, Jackie always painted pointy footprints shaped like a witch's shoes on the classroom floor. The kids would stop short when they saw the prints; their mouths open with surprise.

"Mrs. Reiger! There was a witch! A witch was here!" Then Jackie would explain that the witch must have come in the night and left them candy. Halloween used to be her favorite time of year. Jackie had made Jada's costumes until she had begged for store-bought ones.

Talking about the school kids helped Robert unwind. He and Jackie speculated what the Halloween costumes would be this year. "A few Doc Brown from "Back to the Future," or maybe the mayor in the film, Goldie Wilson," Jackie guessed. "How about one of the kids from 'Goonies.'" She paused. "Except they look like regular kids so that wouldn't be any fun and there was only one girl in Goonies so the girls will probably be Madonna's or Princess Leia's again."

Jackie picked up the shirt and tied off the thread as he talked. Robert told her about the investigation and the visit from Stryker.

"Money seems to motivate these people, but my instinct is that David Emerson's murder was emotional." He leaned back in his chair and took a deep breath to clear his head. "If Stryker would just let me do my job and stop wasting my time, I would be loyal to the guy. But he doesn't act as if he trusts me, so I don't trust him."

"Sergeant Strikeout," Jackie said with disgust. "I hate that guy."

"I know, honey." He patted her arm affectionately. "Your loyalty is my rock." He looked at the shirt she was sewing. "You don't have to do that. I can take it to the laundry."

She shushed him. "You know it keeps my mind occupied."

"You do have a busy mind." He smiled. "A loyal and busy mind."

She gave her husband the side eye and said, "It's not just your run-of-the-mill loyalty I'm carrying. It's a fierce and terrifying one." They laughed. "Now if you're that appreciative—." She set the shirt on the table. "Take me dancing."

"Oh, Jackie." He was about to tell her how beat he felt when the smile on her face changed his mind.

"Okay. Tonight. The Ashkenaz."

15

THE FUNDRAISER

Lexi wore a black velvet dress she had bought at Casual Corner. The asymmetrical skirt flared above the knee. She piled her curly hair up and used combs to secure it, partially. Thick strands of hair cascaded around her head. She hoped it looked sophisticated, but had her doubts. She was late.

Lexi took the bus to California Street and ran, as best she could in heels, to the Fairmont. It sat majestically at the top of Nob Hill overlooking the Marina. The front of the hotel had large flags along the roof above the awning. She heard the ringing of a passing cable car as a uniformed valet swung open the entry doors. A rush of cool air carried her inside.

The lobby was elegant and comfortably furnished. It had vast white marble floors and thick bronze and gold marble columns. *As classical as it gets outside of Rome*, she thought. A large sign read "Welcome, Guests of The Freedom Institute" with an arrow pointing to the ballroom. Lexi was relieved to see the sign since, along with the guest list, she was in charge of signage. She hurried to the large gilded doors and met Renée inside.

"Where have you been?" Renée asked, her demeanor icy.

"I am sorry. It's been such a weird time and the detective—." Lexi stopped short, pretending not to remember his name.

Renée looked down her nose. "Reiger. Detective Robert Reiger."

"He asked me for the guest list cross-referenced with their affiliation with the Institute and with David."

"Mr. Emerson to you." Renée thrust a clipboard with the guest list at Lexi before she turning to walk away. Lexi caught her mid-stride. "Is your husband coming?" Renée turned and smiled broadly, almost too broadly. "He has another engagement in Helsinki."

This was the biggest event the Institute had ever held. The ballroom was massive. Enormous chandeliers gleamed. Tables with centerpieces of large gold vases with white lilies, overhanging greens and baby's breath were surrounded with gold plates. There was a crescendo of white napkin on each plate surrounded by stemware.

Julia was nowhere in sight. Lexi spotted Peggy who called to her. They went over the list. Peggy explained that the author Archie Greenway was to be kept away from her. She was behind and had no idea what was going to happen once the board decided the fate of the Institute.

Peggy was emphatic. "I don't want to outright lie to him and you know Renée will be all over me pushing his project first."

The room started to fill with the buzz of conversation as the wait staff served flutes of champagne and hors d'oeuvres. *Even more glasses,* thought Lexi with a smile.

She was stationed at the entrance. As guests passed her, she was grateful that she recognized most of them and put a checkmark next to their names. It had been drilled into her that asking for a name when they were rich and well-known would be rude.

Before the first event of the year, Lexi looked through *Who's Who* at the library. She also searched back issues of the Institute newsletters to find pictures and put names to faces. They were mostly men. Mary Fairchild was one of the few wealthy women in her own right who hadn't married into money, just inherited it.

Mrs. Amy Davenport Emerson walked in. A hush came over the room. You could hear the classical music that had been masked by the din of conversation. She didn't smile and only nodded to a few of the donors before taking her seat next to Gretchen Stenholm.

Lexi almost gasped. If Amy had killed David, wouldn't she want to kill Gretchen, too? Or, maybe the other way around? There was no way to reach Detective Reiger this late. She decided to pay special attention in case anything happened to either of them. She spotted Grey Neville taking pictures and approached him.

"Grey, would you be sure and get pictures of the head table with Mrs. Emerson?"

"Sure thing," Grey said. It was unusual for Mrs. Emerson to come to Institute events so Grey didn't seem curious about why she had asked.

Gretchen was handsome and wore it well. She was beautifully dressed in flowing emerald green wool slacks and matching jacket. Over her silk blouse and ample breasts a strand of pearls reached her belted waist. She was still tan from the summer and her auburn hair shone with healthy golden highlights from horseback riding—not a hair stylist's coloring job. Lexi had been in her office a few times and noticed pictures of Gretchen riding horses that seemed to gleam with strength and good health.

Mrs. Emerson's wealth, in contrast, showed in her cheekbones and sharp nose that had met with a scalpel. Her blond hair had been sprayed into a protective helmet. The shoulder pads of her magenta jacket jutting into other people's space, she pressed into Gretchen, speaking quietly into her ear.

Just then Archie appeared at the entrance. He was tall and handsome with short, neat hair and skin the color of almonds. He wore glasses and a tailored gray suit with a pink shirt and matching pocket square. When he spied Renée hovering nearby, he made a beeline for her. A bulb flashed. As Lexi's eyes adjusted, Mary Fairchild appeared. All eyes were on her.

"This is going to get interesting," said Julia over Lexi's shoulder. She was holding a glass of wine and smelled of smoke, perfume and alcohol.

"Where have you been?" Lexi asked.

When Julia replied, "None of your beeswax," Lexi must have looked hurt.

"I was talking to a board member," Julia said and pointed her glass toward the back of the room. "They want to set up a meet about the future of the Institute." Julia leaned in closer to Lexi. "The company accounts need addressing before anyone sees them." She took a drink of wine.

Lexi thought, not for the first time, that Julia might have had something to do with David's death. If she thought it, Detective Reiger would as well. Lexi was more determined than ever to find David's killer.

They turned their attention back to Mary. She had shed her fur and leather coat into the arms of an unsuspecting waitress. Her limbs were tan. Her breasts were barely covered by a diaphanous dark blue dress. She teetered on high heels that seemed too small for her feet.

Lexi whispered to Julia, "I *will* fit into these glass slippers." They laughed as Julia drained her drink. Lexi watched and wondered how much more "interesting" things could get.

16

MIDNIGHT

Lexi cut out of the event just after dinner. She was overdressed for the club but didn't want to take the time to change. Switching to flats before leaving the hotel, Lexi caught the cable car to the BART station on Market Street.

Once in Berkeley, Lexi caught a bus down University Avenue, and ran to the Ashkenaz. Cosmo waited outside on San Pablo Avenue. She was so happy to see him. He wore jeans and t-shirt under a faded leather jacket. She hugged him, relieved to be away from the stuffy ballroom where the air was thick with the scent of perfume, hair spray and mothballs.

By 11:00 p.m., they were on the dance floor swaying to Jimmy Cliff singing "Many Rivers to Cross." Lexi had taken her hair down, the curls rising around her head.

Outside the Ashkenaz, middle-aged dealers stood around, ready to sell hard drugs. Detective Robert Reiger sensed danger. He thought it was unusual since he had always known the Ashkenaz to have a laid-back Rasta vibe. There had never been anything harder than pot sold around the club.

Robert put his arm around Jackie as they approached the door. "I don't like how much things have changed around here."

Jackie gave him a gentle shoulder bump. "It's the '80s. Things change."

Robert and the doorman were old friends. They shook hands and pulled each other close for a body hug. "Reiger, man!"

"Jay." Robert looked over his shoulder at the men on the street in front, mingling with patrons cooling off or having a smoke. "What's with the dealers?"

Jay shook his head. "It's been like this for over a year. You haven't been around. We've missed you. But, do me a favor; don't tell Oakland cops to come around. They'll just harass us and arrest anyone who's black." Jay looked weary for a moment before he brightened again. "Where you been?"

"I thought my dancing days were over," Robert said half serious. Jay looked at Jackie who smiled and said, "Not while I draw breath in this body

God gave me." They laughed. Jay hugged Jackie, and Robert nodded with a smile. He shook Jay's hand again and handed over the door charge before following Jackie into the club.

The dance floor was large and crowded. Couples that were not dancing lined the walls. Robert and Jackie made their way to the bar.

Jackie moved her hips to the music as they waited in line. Reiger leaned closer. "I've been working crazy hours. Leaving you home alone." He kissed her neck.

Jackie replied, "Oh, you mean when you get home at seven o'clock because you work a nine-to-five job with no overtime."

Robert smiled. When she was right, she was right. "I just worry. It wasn't this sketchy before. I could get home earlier if we moved to the city. Find a nicer neighborhood. Leave the crime behind."

Jackie looked sad. "This is our home. These are our people." She looked at the sea of Oakland and Berkeley residents with black and brown faces, only a few white people as the minority.

"You know what I'm talking about."

"We are not moving." The look in her eyes was like a period at the end of the sentence. This was where they had raised their daughter, Jada. It would always be their home.

Robert agreed. "We're not moving." He pulled her onto the dance floor. "It was just an idea."

"Oh, was it, now?" She moved in rhythm to the music and let Robert lead her to the middle of the room where they joined the sea of swaying bodies.

The song changed to "Stir It Up." Lexi and Cosmo danced their way around the floor. She recognized the tall burly man. "Detective Reiger is here."

"Who?" asked Cosmo.

"You know, the detective who worked the case." She hesitated but wasn't sure why. "Jerry's case. And he's also on this new one." It sounded strange to be talking about two murder cases. She appreciated how Cosmo didn't press her on either account.

"Oh." Cosmo took Lexi's hand as they moved off the dance floor. He asked, "Do you want to say hello?"

"I do. I have something to tell him."

Lexi led Cosmo through the crowd to where Detective Reiger was standing in line at the bar. His hand rested around the waist of a woman. Lexi thought she looked like a dark-skinned Debbi Morgan from "All My Children." Her cheeks were dimpled even though she wasn't smiling, giving her a friendly look. Her hair was pulled away from her face by a thick headband holding back a luscious Afro. Her large gold hoop earrings almost touched her shoulders.

"Detective Reiger," Lexi yelled just as the music dipped. He turned, along with the woman she assumed was his wife, as did half the people waiting in line.

"Lexi!" Reiger was amused by the commotion. He looked from Lexi to Cosmo.

Lexi said, "This is Cosmo. Cosmo, this is Detective Robert Reiger."

He shook Cosmo's hand and introduced his wife, "Jacqueline Reiger."

"It's so nice to meet you!" Lexi gushed.

A pair of dark cold eyes turned toward Lexi. Jackie didn't extend her hand. Even her dimples had lost their welcoming appeal. Not knowing what else to do, Lexi turned to Reiger and blurted, "Mary Fairchild didn't kill David."

"I know." Reiger said, amused. "I checked her alibi."

"Well," Cosmo pulled Lexi closer. "It was nice to meet you both. We'll see you on the dance floor." He moved them away into the crowd.

Lexi suddenly felt the weight of the long night. She was exhausted. She kissed Cosmo and said, "Let's go."

Outside the club, Robert and Jackie leaned against the wall to cool off. They had been dancing for about two hours. Reiger was feeling it in his cop's feet.

"Your little friend left early," said Jackie.

"You weren't very welcoming."

"We are not going to be friends with that white girl."

"If you got to know her, you'd see she's a little like Jada."

Jackie turned on Robert. "What are you talking about? There is nothing about that girl except maybe her age that is anything like my baby."

Robert let her cool off. She said, "Okay. What is it about—" she paused.

"Lexi Fagan, as you said, is the same age Jada would be. She has an innocence and openness to her. She's pretty clever."

Jackie was unconvinced. "You worked too hard to get where you are. You made no mistakes. You put in more hours than anyone else. What if you're wrong about this girl? What if she's involved in the murder?"

Robert listened. Jackie looked at her husband and said, "Okay. You know what you know. She didn't kill anybody."

Reiger squeezed his wife's hand. "She's never asked me even once if I know Michael Jackson."

Jackie smiled begrudgingly. "Well, that's a first."

A strong wind picked up. "Let's go home. My sweat's starting to cool." As they walked to the car holding hands, she turned to Robert. "She does have that crazy curly hair! But I'm not interested in having that girl in our lives. Just so you know." And with that, tears welled in her eyes. Robert hugged her close, rocking her gently.

She pulled away, looked into his eyes. "I don't have to like her."

"No, you don't." said Robert.

Jackie relented. "I'll cut her some slack. She's just a kid." Robert nodded. He knew his wife well. She had a big heart and was fiercely loyal, two things he loved about her.

With that, she wiped her eyes and straightened her back. As they walked to the car, she pulled Robert's arm tight around her waist.

Lexi and Cosmo had settled in on the futon in her apartment. Bob Dylan's "Lay Lady Lay," played on a portable turntable. Cosmo said, "You know, there was a lot of controversy over Dylan's electric sound. His folk music fans hated it."

"Did they miss his nasally snarl?" Lexi was incredulous before she realized she might have hurt his feelings. "Sorry, you love folk music, right?" He smiled as she sang along in a Dylan-esque voice. "Lay lady lay, lay across my big brass bed."

She leaned into him. "I love this song and this version is the best."

"Don't tell anyone, "said Cosmo, "but I love it, too.

They sang the lyrics "why wait any longer for the world to begin" as they stretched out on the futon, displacing Saxman.

17

IF IT'S SATURDAY, IT'S COSMO

Lexi and Cosmo woke wrapped in each other's arms huddled under the comforter. The air was cold. She leapt out of bed to turn on the heater in the hall. It kept the hall warm but not much else. She crawled back into bed and tried to adjust her body around Saxman. Disgusted, she jumped off the bed.

Lexi snuggled next to Cosmo. As he roused from a deep sleep they made love again. Her body responded but her mind was elsewhere. She had been confused by Jackie's coldness. She pushed that thought away, leaving something more pressing to think about. What was Julia hiding?

Lexi's laced her second-hand roller skates. She had grown out of them a long time ago but didn't use them enough to justify a new pair. There was not even a place to roller skate in Ketchikan. Her grandparents must have read somewhere that roller skates were a present 12-year-olds wanted for Christmas.

She and Cosmo drove to the park in his beat-up MG. It was not as crowded as it had been during the heyday of roller disco in the 1970s. Cosmo told Lexi about the roller skate truck rentals along Fulton Avenue. The city had closed several blocks in Golden Gate Park just for skaters. There had been thousands of people. He had told her that you could hear competing disco music playing from every direction on JFK Drive. Today, the park closed off only a few streets and there were only a handful of skaters.

Cosmo's blades were brand-new. He was already skating circles around Lexi as she put on her skates. She had not dressed for the weather— just jeans, a cotton sweater and a short leather jacket. She shivered as she sat on the concrete to adjust her laces.

Lexi and Cosmo skated to the edge of a group of teenagers. They were dressed in less than she. No coats. Tight jeans. Long feather and bead earrings that stuck to their long bushy hair. The teen boys had long hair as well, short on top and long in the back.

A handsome dark-skinned skater with a boom box resting on his shoulder skated past them, his movements smooth and even. "Not his first time," Cosmo said. They watched in admiration before skating faster to keep up. Billy Ocean's "Caribbean Queen" played as he disappeared around a corner.

Losing her footing, Lexi tumbled over. Her knee hit hard. Her jeans were ripped, exposing the skin underneath. Asphalt ground into the open wound. Cosmo sprang into action, righted Lexi into a seated position to assess the damage.

"I'm fine." Lexi tried to stand up. She brushed the gravel out of her bloody knee. It hurt like mad, but she didn't want him to fuss.

"Let me help you," he pleaded.

"It's fine."

"It's my job even if I wasn't your boyfriend." He sounded hurt.

Lexi fought back tears from the pain and frustration. She didn't want him to see her like this. She didn't want to need him.

"You're scraped up bad." He looked at her. "Why won't you let me help you?"

"I said I was fine." She started skating away. Blood oozed from her knee.

Bewildered, Cosmo followed.

The ramshackle Sausalito dock stretched away from the freeway that led travelers further into

Marin County. Cosmo's neighbors were friendly,
open, hippie-types who had dropped out to live
as close to nature as they could afford.

Lexi and Cosmo spent many weekends together on his boat. She felt bad leaving Saxman, and
had tried to get Cosmo to come to the city more
often. He preferred his small but neat home on
the water to her messy studio apartment on Russian Hill.

That night, Lexi accepted pain medication and
reluctantly allowed Cosmo to clean her knee.
Something in her still made it hard to accept
help. It had started after Paula had attacked her.
Lexi had thought of her as a friend. She had dis-
covered Paula and Paula's lover Trevor had killed
Jerry and had been intent on killing her as well.
If it had not been for Ben, she would have been
their next victim. She had taken self-defense classes, but Ben was still the only person she felt truly
safe around.

"I'm just trying to clean the wound so you
don't get an infection." Lexi sat on the bed next
to Cosmo. "I am a professional."

"I know. I am sorry. I'm starting to feel as
if I'm bad luck. First Jerry and now Mr. Emerson."

Cosmo kissed her. "You aren't bad luck."

"It feels strange to have someone, you know?"

"I understand. You've been through a lot but if you don't let your guard down—" his words trailed off. He stood up. "Let me make dinner."

He opened his tiny fridge and took out the ingredients for shrimp linguini with cream sauce. He opened the carton of cream and smelled it.

"This might be bad." He handed the carton to Lexi. "Try this."

She laughed. "You always ask me to try bad food. If it smells—" she stopped to take a whiff. "Eww. It's off." She handed the carton back. "You can trust your own nose."

"This is not a problem." He set the carton in the sink, grabbed the olive oil and covered the bottom of the saucepan with oil. "Linguini with shrimp and olive oil."

18

GREY NEVILLE

Detective Reiger often spent time in book-stores in Oakland and Berkeley on Sundays after church. He would leave Jackie to visit with friends sitting in the church basement in the winter or in the garden in summer, their magnificent hats forming a rainbow of bright feathers and flowers.

Today, at Pendragon on College Avenue, Reiger noticed a small slight man, light-skinned. He was dressed like a professor, complete with elbow patches on his jacket sleeves. Reiger thought his long Afro could use a comb-out, but he recognized him. It was Grey Neville, Peggy's husband, the rare book dealer.

He put down the book he had been considering and approached Grey. "Mr. Grey Neville." Extending his hand, he said, "Detective Robert Reiger, San Francisco Homicide."

Grey shook his hand with surprising strength.

"Yes. Yes. It's me," he stammered, the nerd coming through. He released Reiger's hand and took a step back. "So you're a homicide detective. Well, I'll be. I've seen you around Moe's and Black Oak but never guessed you were a cop." As if remembering he had a pan on the stove, Grey suddenly jumped. "Oh! You're! You're! Investigating David Emerson's death."

Reiger smiled at how animated and cheerful Grey seemed despite the topic.

"That's right, Mr. Neville."

"Grey. Call me Grey."

"Grey is an interesting name."

"You've got me there Detective," Grey said smiling.

Reiger asked, "What did your mama say about changing your name?"

"The Gladys? She took some convincing."

"I bet." They laughed long and hard. Finally, Grey said, "My born name is Tyrone Jackson, but I couldn't get anywhere in this old-book business with that name. So I changed it to Grey."

"It does have a British country squire ring to it." Reiger shook his head. "And Neville?"

"The Neville Brothers of course."

A sly smile crossed Reiger's lips. "I'd like to ask you about The Freedom Institute."

"Sure! There's no undiscovered treasure buried under these old books. I don't know why I bother. These guys—" Grey swept his hand toward the cash register and the disheveled clerk with a long greasy ponytail—"know to grab them before the professionals start sniffing around."

They found a seat at the café next to the bookstore. Reiger drank his tea and watched as the spirited book dealer sipped a large cup of black coffee.

"How do you know David Emerson?"

"It bothers me that he had a literary name. Emerson. Ralph Waldo Emerson."

"I take it you didn't like him?" Reiger was talking slowly to bring down Grey's energy.

"David! He was a numbskull! But a real gangster. You know what I mean?"

Reiger's steady gaze had the desired effect. Grey's voice dropped an octave. "May he rest in peace."

"Tell me about the first edition of *Atlas Shrugged* you procured for Mr. Emerson." Reiger watched for a reaction but none came.

Grey was silent for a long while. "I didn't know anyone knew about that. It was a gift. I saw it and knew David would want it. He was giving me work and I wanted to thank him."

"Photographs."

"Yeah." Grey leaned back and looked at Reiger. "You know a lot."

"It is a murder investigation."

Grey laughed nervously. "Of course. I should have been more respectful."

Reiger shook it off. "Not many people seem to have liked David Emerson."

"Libertarians. They can be charming when it comes to social issues. If you're gay, they don't care. If you're an immigrant or want to do drugs, they could not care less, but if you're poor, it's your own fault. And don't stop them from making money with pesky regulations." Grey drained his cup. "Why would anyone need protecting from business? They always have your best interest at heart." His voice dripped with sarcasm.

"How much did you pay for the Rand book?"

"It's not that rare. It's only, what? 28 years old." Grey shifted in his seat. "It was maybe a hundred dollars. I'm sure David intended to sell it later to a donor. Even the biggest donors had to buy things like that from David. The Mary Fairchilds and the Clark brothers basically keep the lights on at The Freedom Institute. David would sell the book to one of them."

Reiger asked, "Does it rile you that David raises millions for books that nobody reads?"

Grey reached into his book-bag and took out a plain, worn book. "Know what this is? It's a second edition of *My Bondage and My Freedom*. He handed it to Reiger who looked at it in awe.

Reiger was impressed. "Frederick Douglass." He handed the book back to Grey. "So David's commercialism did upset you."

Grey looked around to check that no one had overheard him talk about his treasure. "No. I never cared what David did. I'm not like my wife. To be a libertarian, she has to convince herself there's a finite amount of wealth in the world. I don't buy it. I love her, but she is mixed up in the head about some things. And bless her, she lets me be me."

Reiger said, "I gathered that Peggy is a true believer."

"Oh, yes." Grey started to perk up again. "She's the most loyal person. I think she hated David but wouldn't talk bad about him to a stranger. She believes in free will, don't tread on me, the whole nine yards." He paused. Reiger raised an eyebrow.

"Yes," he answered the unasked question. "Peggy comes from money. Old-world money. It's almost gone now, but it made her ripe for the mother of libertarianism, Ayn Rand. It's as if you have to come from a communist country or be rich to go all in. There's doesn't seem to be an in-between."

Reiger looked at his watch. "Listen—" He stood and extended his hand to Grey. "I appreciate your time. I'll be in touch." They shook hands. "I need to pick up my wife at church."

Grey smiled. "That sounds about right."

As Reiger walked down College Avenue, he thought how Grey had not been straight with him. The book in David's office would not have cost that little. He also suspected that it had not been a gift. He would need to look at the Nevilles' bank records.

19

L exi woke to the gentle rocking of the Sea Worthy. It was 6:00 a.m. and she needed to hustle to make the 6:45 ferry to San Francisco. She packed her book-bag, checking that the fireman's badge that Jerry's mother had given her at his memorial was in the front pocket. She took it out and rubbed it as she did every morning.

Cosmo was still asleep. She kissed him and walked to the Taste of Rome. Her book-bag felt particularly heavy this morning. It had clothes, her work shoes, a book to read on the ferry and her toothbrush. Cosmo had asked her to leave her things, but she did not want to leave pieces of her life in other places.

She grabbed a latte and walked briskly to the dock and onto the boat. She loved standing on deck as the ferry moved slowly toward the city.

Today, it was freezing. Her work uniform of a jacket, skirt, tights and boots wasn't cutting it. She watched Coit Tower and the Transamerica Building come into view.

Standing under the shadow of the Embarcadero Freeway, San Francisco's ferry terminal was located in a sketchy area of town. As she walked down the ramp to the dock, Lexi stuck close to the group disembarking the ferry on their way to work. As she walked toward the cable car outside a hotel on Market Street, Lexi heard the familiar ranting of the regular who sat on the bench.

Henry had told her that the man was Maxon Crumb, cartoonist R. Crumb's brother. As she passed the bench, his wild eyes landed on her for a second before moving on. His restless body swayed as he screamed. None of the commuters paid attention to him. There were street people you could approach and give food to and some you could not. Maxon was a no.

Once at the office, Lexi started her routine. She opened the window in Julia's office and took her cup to the kitchen. As she watched the liquid go down the drain, she felt a shift. There was no need to keep Julia's secret. David was gone. Everyone else knew. She dried the cup. A sense of relief washed over her. She would try and help Julia stop drinking.

She heard the front door open. Detective Reiger was in the reception area. It was warm in the office. He said hello, took off his jacket and sat on the couch, smoothing the leather of the coat next to him. It had been five days since David had been murdered. Lexi could see the strain on Reiger's face. She looked at the clock, 9:10 a.m. Plenty of time to talk before the rest of the staff arrived.

"I need to get back to motive. Why kill David?"

Lexi considered. "What I've learned over the past week—." She stopped to take a breath. "Is that David was awful."

"Was he awful to you?"

"That's the thing. He had nothing to hold over me. I was too low on the totem pole." Lexi thought for a minute. "Here's a typical David move. He asked me to sharpen his pencils when I was in the middle of reconciling donor lists. I ran into his office and grabbed the pencil cup. I set them on my desk so I could finish the list Julia was waiting for. He walked up to me, crossed his arms and literally stood over me, waiting for me to sharpen the pencils. I was so mad. I sharpened each one, walked into his office and dumped them onto his desk."

Reiger asked. "What did he do?"

"He shrugged."

"Not a complete jerk, then?"

"Okay. He gets a tiny bit of credit."

"There has to be more. He was a complicated man." Reiger waited.

"I'm sure you noticed the pictures of donors in his office? We switch the photos depending on who was visiting David."

"There was a lot of switching going on." Reiger mused. "Like with his lovers."

Just then, Julia breezed in carrying a bushy fern. "For your desk," she said, setting it down with a flourish. Surprised, Lexi stammered a thank you.

Julia smiled at Reiger. "The great thing about a plant—unlike some people we knew" —she tilted her head toward David's office—"is when plants stop producing oxygen, you can throw them away."

Lexi suppressed a laugh. Julia walked down the hall to her office as Reiger sat back down. "She's a character. Now, let's start at the beginning. What other subterfuge was David up to?"

Lexi said. "There's more, about David and donors. You know he liked to impress people."

"Go on."

"He lied about that, too. The diploma in his office? It's not real. He had Jack mock them up." Lexi opened a drawer and took out a stack of framed diplomas from Dartmouth and Harvard. "Depending on the donor he was wooing." She stacked the frames on her desk.

"How did you keep track of all the lies?"

"I have a spreadsheet. We researched where the donors had graduated and that diploma gets pride of place."

Reiger shook his head. "That seems like a risk. They could easily have looked him up and found he wasn't an alumnus."

"Well, that was David. If anyone had thought to ask, he would have talked rings around them. But I don't remember anyone ever following up. The people that give money here are very wealthy. They're into themselves."

Instead of putting the frames back in the desk drawer, she stacked them in the garbage can.

"I won't miss him." Lexi suddenly started to cry. She wiped her eyes with the back of her hand in anger. "I don't know why I'm blubbering. I didn't think to tell you about all the ways David got money out of people. It was just the way we did things."

Reiger took a handkerchief from his pocket and handed it to her. "This situation is bringing up a lot of loss."

Lexi squared her shoulders and shook her head. She said, "I can't help thinking David's murder has to do with the books and not the lovers."

Reiger nodded. "You might be right. I'm interviewing Mrs. Davenport Emerson this afternoon. That should clarify things."

"The grieving widow."

Reiger gave Lexi a concerned look. "Forgive yourself for not telling me about the diplomas. I don't think he was murdered for that." He stood. "Don't dismiss your feelings. They have a way of coming back no matter how much you push them down." He gave Lexi a fatherly nod. "I'm going to interview Julia." He disappeared down the hall as Renée walked in. Lexi noticed her suit matched the burgundy of the office carpet. Instead of breezing past her as usual, Renée stopped at Lexi's desk and picked up a framed photo. "You can tell a lot from a photograph."

Lexi asked, "What do you see?"

"Well, I'll tell you. It's of a cat," she scoffed. "Most people would have pictures of their family or vacations with college roommates or I'd even accept your boyfriend what's-his-name."

Lexi did not bite. Renée knew Cosmo's name. She took the photo from Renée and put it back on the desk. Renée glanced at the computer screen. "I'll tell you this. You misspelled *laissez-faire.*"

Lexi snapped, "I didn't go to a fancy prep school like you." Her face burned with anger and embarrassment.

"Not to worry." Renée said, looking satisfied. "You make up for it in other ways."

"I felt the back hand of your compliment." Tired of feeling intimidated by Renée, Lexi had practiced that line for months. It wasn't the best time to use it, but she was angry and provoked.

Then, Renée did something unexpected. She laughed.

Reiger could smell wine on Julia even this early in the morning. He would need to talk to Lexi about why she had kept the information about this level of drinking from him. Jack had not been exaggerating, but it should have come from Lexi. Jack had also been right about how well put-together Julia was. Reiger's intuition was that she dressed to perfection because she felt great shame that the drinking was getting the better of her.

The cloying scent of perfume and lingering scent of alcohol were like a shield around her. Reiger sat down. On the desk was a coffee cup with white liquid. She must have a bottle stashed somewhere. She pointed to the pack of smokes neatly squared in the corner of the tidy desk. He nodded since the window was open. She lit and inhaled deeply.

Reiger asked, "What happens now? Does The Freedom Institute stay open?"

"Of course." Julia seemed surprised by the question. "Jack's writing a press release about

David. We had a book launch and fundraising event Friday. Business as usual."

"You run on donations, correct?" Julia nodded. He continued, "Tell me how the money flows."

Julia pulled a ledger from a drawer and opened it. "It's all here. We raise money for specific projects, mostly books, sometimes for scholarly research."

"What about David leaving Reed? Any resentment about that?"

"Nothing that would get him killed. It's normal to strike out on your own. You know, free market philosophy?"

Reiger gave her a look.

"Yes, of course you do. Reed wouldn't want the competition for donors but had to accept it. It's their core philosophy so they couldn't openly resent it when David opened The Freedom Institute, but, of course, they were pissed." She took a long drag and blew the smoke toward the window. "One reason David left was that Reed moved to Washington to maximize their lobbying efforts. David's wife would have loved to move back east, but he always did what he wanted."

"You need to be more specific."

"I'm sure you noticed David's graying temples?" Reiger nodded. She continued. "Well, that was David. He wanted respect. The beautiful wife and kids in pictures on his desk. He had what he wanted." She paused. "Until Mary."

"Do you think Amy Davenport Emerson would kill her husband?"

"She might. David humiliated her." She tried to steer the conversation elsewhere. "Are you a follower of Ayn Rand?"

"Meaning?"

Julia shifted in her seat. Reiger said, "This is a murder investigation. If you aren't honest with me, I will find out and charge you with obstruction."

She lowered her voice though the door was closed. "He didn't always use the money that was meant for a book *for* the book, if you know what I mean."

"What does that have to do with Rand?"

"There's a certain bending of the rules." Julia unlocked a large bottom drawer in her desk and pulled out a second ledger. "Ends justifying the means." She set the ledger in front of Reiger on top of the other set of books.

"It's all there."

Reiger opened the ledger as Julia continued. "See—." She stood and walked around the desk to stand next to Reiger's chair. She traced an entry along a line. "Money is allocated for a particular book, production begins and then it disappears on one ledger and appears on the other."

She moved the first book and opened the second before continuing. "This entry shows the book printed and ready for a launch party."

"Here," she returned to the first ledger. "The money goes into David's secret off-shore account." She sat back down. "Gotta love the Swiss."

"Who else knows about this besides you?"

"No one that I know of. This drawer is always locked. Every accounting meeting we had took place at the Iron Horse. You know, in Maiden Lane?" She didn't wait for Reiger to answer. "David didn't trust anyone, maybe because he wasn't above spying."

"He spied on his own people?"

"He knew everything that happened here."

Reiger wondered if David had known about Jack's double-dealing but didn't want that information floating around. As he stood to leave, he said, "David sounds like a real mensch," bringing a smile to Julia's lips. He picked up the ledgers. "I'm taking these."

In the reception area, Reiger addressed Lexi. "I know about Julia and her serious drinking problem. You can't keep information from me. I thought you understood that, but I must have failed you somehow." Lexi looked away, ashamed. He said, "I trusted you."

She felt sick.

"This isn't a game, Lexi." He took a deep breath and looked at his watch. "I'm due at the lab. Do not do anything heroic to try and solve this case to get back in my good graces." He walked to the door but turned around. "We can talk about this later."

20

MRS. AMY DAVENPORT EMERSON

The Emerson house was a large, white colonial with views of what remained of the Sutro Baths, a site resembling ancient ruins on the cliffs that overlooked the Pacific Ocean. Below the Sutro Baths sat the old Cliff House restaurant with a view of Seal Rock, perched on the edge of the earth. Cypress trees straining their branches fought with the wind, obscuring much of the view from the Emerson home. Reiger could hear the barking of seals sunbathing on Seal Rock. He was standing in the spacious living room.

"It's called Land's End. I've never liked it. I'm from the east coast. This is a bit Barbary Coast for my taste. It's usually foggy and cold out here." Amy Davenport Emerson sank into her seat, staring out the picture window. "The seals' incessant

yammering makes me want to take my head off."
She paused. "Or theirs." She gave Reiger a look as
if to gauge his reaction.

Reiger walked to the window facing the yard
at the side of the house. "It's sunny today and you
have a lovely garden. Should we continue our talk
outside?"

"I suppose so."

Reiger looked at pictures on the fireplace
mantle. Each silver-framed picture was professional, posed. The twins wore long christening
gowns. "Will the children be all right?"

"My mother's upstairs. She's watching the
twins during this trying time."

They walked through large intricately pat-
terned leaded glass doors into the lush garden.
Once outside, Reiger and Mrs. Davenport Emerson sat on uncomfortable wrought iron chairs
with a small table between them. The garden had
beds of ferns with wide fronds, tasteful camellia
bushes and rows of well-tended roses.

Reiger looked from the garden to David's
wife. "Mrs. Emerson—"

She cut him off. "I'm a Davenport. Davenport
Emerson."

Reiger smiled at the correction. "Mrs. Davenport Emerson, you didn't report your husband
missing. Weren't you concerned when he didn't
come home?"

"No," she said flatly. "David has an apartment downtown near the office. Oh, the car—." She shifted in her seat. "There's a garage at the apartment."

"Can you give me the address and a key? We'll need access to the apartment and to his car."

"Why? Wasn't he killed at work?"

"Mrs. Davenport Emerson," Reiger looked at her with kindness. "I am so very sorry for your loss, but this is a murder investigation. We have to look at David's movements that night."

"Tea!?" Mrs. Davenport Emerson rose and moved toward the French doors. She turned as if to add something, but changed her mind.

Reiger had witnessed many responses to sudden death and wasn't surprised at a recently widowed wife, with twin babies, unable to focus on the aftermath. What he was surprised about was her good timing.

He said, "thank you" for the offer of tea. As she disappeared inside, Reiger stood up to look around the garden for what he had come to find. It was unusually warm for late October. Earthquake weather. Reiger didn't want to take off his leather jacket. He wasn't going to stay long. He wiped his brow with a handkerchief that had been his grandfather's, folded it carefully and put it back in his jacket pocket. He walked the short distance to a shaded area under a thick stand of purple bayhops and found a small colony of mushrooms. He scooped several into an evidence bag and put them in his pocket, returning to his seat. The damp ocean air reminded him of his mother's house in the Sunset District that was so often socked in with fog.

Mrs. Davenport Emerson came out with a tray filled with a beautiful Chinese tea set.

"It's the maid's day off," she said apologetically.

After she poured the tea, Reiger took a sip of the Darjeeling. Unless you were in Chinatown, this quality of tea was rare. Despite wanting to leave because of the heat and the mushrooms and needing to get to the lab, he lingered to finish his tea.

"What do you think of your husband's work?"

"Libertarianism? It's stale. No matter how many books and publications and pamphlets and crap they put out, it's as if their intellectual curiosity stopped at Ayn Rand. They never move on to embrace other philosophies that might improve upon theirs. It's in desperate need of an overhaul."

Reiger was surprised by her down-to-earth response. "Maybe start with their lack of ethics, perhaps?"

"More like a blindness to how capitalism without regulation always hurts the environment or worker's health, suppresses wages or just plain squeezes the hell out of the markets." She un-crossed her legs as she turned to ask, politely, "More tea, Detective?"

Reiger nodded. It was time to get down to business. "How well do you know Mary Fairchild?"

"I couldn't pick her out of a line-up."

Reiger gave a wry laugh. "Is that true?"

"I wish it were."

"You knew about the affair." It was a statement not a question.

"I did and I hated David for it, but I wouldn't kill him. You must believe me." Though her words were passionate, her demeanor didn't crack. She had been more animated about the state of liber-tarianism.

Reiger continued his line of inquiry. "And when did you find out about Gretchen and Da-vid?"

The fog began to roll gently over the garden. Only the barking of seals and the cry of seagulls broke the silence.

21

LORD OF THE FLIES

B ack at the Institute, Lexi had recovered her composure by splashing water on her face. She did have divided loyalty and should have been honest with Detective Reiger about Julia's alcoholism. She had not been honest with herself about it. The co-dependent bond between them was strong. She still felt heartsick that Reiger thought he had "failed her," but hoped that she could regain his trust by following his advice.

Peggy entered the bathroom as Lexi was wiping her face and, typically oblivious to Lexi's state, she asked her to come to her house and review the photos from the fundraiser with Grey.

Peggy spoke freely. "It should be Renée choosing what pictures to use, but I can't stand to listen to her go on about *her* writers anymore. It drives

Grey nuts, too. Unfortunately, I can write my way out of anything, but I can't pick a good photo to save my life. And Grey's no help. He won't make any decisions. It's as if each picture is a "Sophie's Choice." You've got to help me out."

"Won't Renée be angry you aren't asking her?"

"Who cares?" she answered dismissively.

Lexi thought it was already like the *Lord of the Flies* at the office. Who thought things could get even more chaotic without David at the helm?

22

THE NEVILLE HOME

The time leading up to and including Halloween was a delight for Lexi to experience in San Francisco. It was the city's true holiday, when the entire community could show off and party in the streets. It was more fabulous-treat than scary-trick as gays, straights, business people, hippies, and suburban and city kids played together. It was St. Patrick's Day on steroids. This year, though, Lexi couldn't enjoy the ghouls, spiders and bats hanging in the windows of the Italian restaurants, coffee houses and bookstores along Columbus Avenue.

Back at her apartment, she petted Saxman absently while eating cold Chinese food out of the carton. She left the dregs for a disappointed Saxman before throwing on jeans and a leather jacket and heading to Berkeley. She was relieved to have something to do. It would keep her from feeling like the loser who disappointed Reiger, a person she respected and genuinely liked.

Peggy and Grey's house was on a tree-lined street in north Berkeley. Large oak leaves were scattered on the sidewalk. It was dark with only dim streetlights. They lived in a Craftsman home with a wide stone porch under a shingled roof. Lexi climbed the front stairs and could see the living room through the picture window. Stuffed bookshelves dominated the room. There was an old couch covered in blankets and funky pillows and a large wooden coffee table also covered in books, magazines and newspapers. Lexi again thought how the room looked warm and inviting, if a bit chaotic.

Lexi had been at the Nevilles' home for a birthday party for Grey over the summer. Things had not improved in the neatness department.

The door was unlocked and she walked inside. She called to Peggy who answered from the kitchen. Lexi walked the hallway lined with more bookshelves bulging with some of the most beautiful books Lexi had ever seen. She had not dared to touch the books during the party, but something inside her felt unmoored now. Rules seemed meant to be broken. She lingered, touching the spines when Peggy's voice reached her again. "Don't touch those books! They're worth a king's ransom."

Lexi stepped into the kitchen. Peggy was at the table thumbing through a magazine. The dishwasher was either broken or was full or both. Dishes and glasses overflowed in the sink. The kitchen table—a long rustic picnic table with benches—was covered with abandoned coffee cups sitting on top of magazines and journals.

"It's a mess in here," said Peggy sweeping her arm in front of her. "Let's go to Grey's office." She handed Lexi a short water glass filled with red wine and motioned for her to follow. "Not that it's much better in there," she said over her shoulder.

They passed through the living room. As they walked, Lexi noticed the modern art that looked as if it were original works and not inexpensive prints. Once they reached Grey's office, Peggy hugged her husband. He hugged her back with such affection it made Lexi yearn for that close-ness. She remembered hugging Jerry that way.

Noticing her, Grey greeted her warmly. "Thanks for coming. I enjoy Renée's perfection-ism as much as the next guy," he gave her a mis-chievous smile. "But it drives Peggy nuts, so I'm glad you're here. Let's dive in." Peggy left them to it.

The room was neater than the rest of the house, but that wasn't saying much. An oak desk anchored one side of the office. Large prints, some in frames and some on pressboard, were stacked against two of the other walls. Shelves were lined with more prints, old cameras, African statuary and masks next to books and film canisters along the fourth wall. There was a window above the desk looking into the overgrown yet charming back yard. A set of carved mahogany lion heads held what looked like the oldest of the books.

Lexi picked up a gilt-edged book in the center and turned it over in her hands.

"Oh, my dear." Grey took the book gently, leafing through the pages. "That is a wonderful book of writings for Cleopatra by her lover Mark Antony." He set it down and continued dreamily, "Tragic, tragic love. People will do anything for love and often shed buckets of tears in the process."

Grey seemed to wake from his reverie. "At least in books."

"Is it rare?" asked Lexi.

"Love?"

She laughed. "No, the book?"

"Not at all. I just like it." Grey set it aside.

They were standing by a metal display cabinet with old books behind glass. Next to it was a drafting table with sheets of black and white photographs taken at the fundraiser. Grey motioned for her to follow him. He handed her a loupe.

"These are the contact sheets. You see there are rows of pictures on each page. Every photo on the roll of film from the event is here. You'll be marking the best shots with this red pencil." He handed her a wax pencil. The pencil was wrapped in paper like a crayon that was unfurled to expose a fresh edge. Grey showed her a marked-up proof sheet with six images across and five down. Three of the photos had been circled in red.

Lexi scanned the sheets. "These are beautiful." She noticed that Grey focused on one detail when composing a shot, a gleaming glass of champagne or a particularly elaborate necklace.

Lexi took the top sheet on a stack and started marking the best pictures. Grey did the same. They made it through a few pages when Grey froze and gasped.

"What is it?" she asked.

"Oh," he said recovering. "Nothing. I thought I had a lens flare in the middle of the best shot of the guest of honor. But, it's not that bad. I'll need to work in the dark room to fix it." He quickly put the sheet aside, covering it with a sheet of paper. Lexi had glanced at the images as he picked it up. They were a series of shots from the main table. She could just make out Gretchen and Amy seated together. The dinner plates were cleared so it must have been when Julia had disappeared just before Mary Fairchild walked in. Grey was acting a bit squirrelly. She thought for a split second that he might be hiding something.

They returned to the task and spent the next hour marking shots of donors talking, raising toasts to the guest of honor, the economist Milton Freeman, and two good shots of Archie Greenway talking with donors to show "diversity." The idea gave Grey and Lexi a good laugh.

"The last time Renée was here, she had a hissy fit that we hadn't featured Archie more. She's very proud of him."

"Proud? Why?"

"You mean besides the fact that he's black and that's as rare as a unicorn in libertarian circles?"

"There is that," Lexi said, smiling.

Grey paused, staring at the sheet he was working on. "He's a good writer and she promised him publication before The Reed Foundation could lure him away."

"If Peggy's backed up and he's a good writer, why didn't David just agree to have Archie write his own book?"

Grey put down the proof sheet. "I don't know. What I do know is that Renée won't stop going on about it. That's why I didn't want her here choosing the pictures. Besides, you're more fun."

Lexi couldn't let that pass. "I'm confused."

"There's a lot you don't know about the Institute."

She wanted to know everything. "Did you sell David a first edition of *Atlas Shrugged?*" Grey seemed surprised by the question. "Detective Reiger asked me the same thing." He glanced down the hall to see if Peggy was in earshot. He whispered, "The truth is that David asked me to pick up the book for him and then he had the nerve to pretend it was a donation!"

"You must have been upset."

"That's putting it mildly." His shoulders slumped. "I couldn't come right out and accuse him of stealing. What if he took it out on my wife?"

"I don't understand libertarian books. I've worked there for over a year and don't get what they believe in. I'm unclear what they feel so oppressed by. Freedom from what, exactly?"

Grey straightened his shoulders again. He seemed happy to educate her. "Let me elucidate. In a nutshell, libertarians don't want to pay taxes or be restricted from making money with pesky regulations. That's what they mean by free market. It's called unfettered capitalism. The triumph of individualism. The opposite of the collective good."

"All that money spent on publishing books and papers because they don't want to pay taxes?" Lexi paused. "Is that why they don't care about social issues?" She felt as if had gotten mixed up in some kind of economic cult. How could she have been so uninterested in what the Institute stood for?

"Exactly," Grey said. "It's nice to talk to someone openly since Peggy will hear no critique of her favorite philosophy. I read *Atlas Shrugged* in high school. I thought it was poorly written. I hated the characters and the plot was preposterous. Peggy had the opposite reaction. She was deeply affected by it and, for those like her, it became a religion.

Lexi nodded, wanting to hear more.

"When the rationalists took religion away, men just found another religion. Libertarianism." Grey was on a roll. "Socialism is a religion. Even Communism is a religion. Their beliefs are doctrine to them, but the same is true for the other side. The believers think that government can save people, fix anything. It's another form of zealotry. People need to believe in something."

"Isn't everything about competition?" Lexi asked.

"Well, not always. People have misinterpreted Darwin to prove that nature is a constant battle for dominance. You've heard of 'survival of the fittest.'"

Lexi nodded.

"Well, that's not the whole picture. What Darwin observed was adaptation. Nature adapts to its environment and not always by one-upping their peers. There's a game theory about how hawks and doves, two adversaries in nature, have been observed cooperating."

Lexi's eyes narrowed.

"Stay with me here." Grey was animated. "The game theory shows that survival of the fittest is wrong because animals don't always do it. A bird might cry out to warn that a top predator is coming. You see, the bird will call out and warn all creatures even though their chances of being killed and eaten are higher by sounding the alarm and drawing attention to themselves."

Lexi shook her head. "I don't really get it, but don't give up. I do want to understand." She was glad that Grey was telling her what he really thought. She guessed he felt more comfortable now that there was no way for gossip to get back to David.

Grey's face lit up as he talked. "The bottom line is that there are a lot of examples of cooperation between species that don't include kill-or-be-killed models." He looked toward the window and took a deep breath. "I got off track. I think libertarians are greedy bastards who use competition to crush others without thinking about the health of the entire system. And I believe in adaptation. On the other hand, I understand Archie's approach that economics is the key to African American mobility." The words flooded out of him. "There's some writing by Frederick Douglass where he agreed with the idea that handouts aren't good—but then again, others say he just wanted the government to enforce the laws that make blacks equal economic partners on the same footing as whites, and then handouts wouldn't be needed. Let us prosper!"

He paused for a breath. "So, there's an appeal for Archie and others like him, but the fact that there are so few black libertarians proves there are barriers beyond economics—" Grey stopped. "I am rambling."

He looked at Lexi as if he had just noticed she wasn't following his discourse and said, "What do you believe in?"

Lexi thought for a long time before throwing her hands in the air in defeat. "I don't know."

"Believe in love," he said as Peggy came into the room. "It's a good one. Isn't that right, my love?"

"Is Grey boring you with obscure game theory?"

"I think it's amazing," Lexi gushed.

Peggy turned to her husband. "The problem with big governments is that they interfere with your life. It's intrusive and steps on my right to life, liberty and the pursuit of happiness."

Grey leaned closer to Lexi and whispered, "Pursuit of money is more like it."

Peggy shot him a look. Lexi knew that money was a sore spot. Grcy said, "I know. Money is important, but corporations screw up. At least the government—and we are talking about people here not Orwellian '1984' faceless bureaucrats—are public servants and with the right checks and balances, corruption can be lessened and governments can help people."

"I don't want their help." Peggy said with a stern face, but her voice was warm. Grey pulled her close. "Fair enough." Peggy returned his hug and smiled at Lexi.

As interesting as their conversation was, it was getting late and Lexi wasn't going to make it home in time for her 6:00 p.m. call with Cosmo. On her way to the North Berkeley BART station, she stopped at a phone booth and waited the 5 minutes until 6:00 before dialing the number of the phone booth where Cosmo would be standing in Sausalito.

As soon as Cosmo picked up, she started to cry. She told him how she had disappointed Reiger and how disappointed she was in herself. He let her cry until they heard the operator ask for more coins. She fumbled for a quarter and put it in the slot.

"It's just that I don't know if Julia is covering up for something that David did—" she sobbed. Catching her breath, she continued,

"And Reiger has been great to me always. He even said I remind him of his daughter—." She could not stop crying, snot clogged her nose. "And she's gone!"

"Who's gone?" Cosmo asked gently.

"Jada!"

23

OAKLAND

At Robert Reiger's home, the dinner dishes had been cleared and The Freedom Institute ledgers were sitting on the kitchen table. He didn't want to be as late getting home as he had been every night since the investigation started, but bringing work home had not pleased Jackie. He reminded her she had grading to do.

Jackie shook her head. "Yes, I do bring work home."

"I don't mind. You love what you do and, despite Stryker, I love my job, too."

She reached across the table and squeezed his hand. "What are these?" she indicated the books.

"Motive." He sighed. "Suspects are multiplying by the minute."

"Except your pet." Reiger saw the twinkle in Jackie's eye when she teased him. He was relieved that she had let it go. She stood. "I'll leave you to it."

Reviewing the numbers on the balance sheets, Robert's suspicions were confirmed. The books were proof that David Emerson had been embezzling huge sums from his own company from the start. He also noted that neither set of books showed a payment to Grey Neville for a first edition of *Atlas Shrugged*. Earlier in the day, Reiger had called a friend in the book business that confirmed that a first edition of that book would be worth thousands in the libertarian world.

He made one last mental note before closing the books: Jack made almost twice Peggy's salary.

24

The long, stainless steel counter at Dr. Yu's lab had white containers lined with vials, a centrifuge machine and two microscopes. Reiger looked at Dr. Yu peering at a test tube. "Where did you find these babies?" Yu asked.

"Under an Ipomoea pes-caprae bush." He paused for effect. "In Mrs. Amy Davenport Emerson's garden."

"Ah, bayhops. Goat's foot. A good plant to grow mushrooms under," Yu scoffed. "So, it was the wife. I told you it was a woman." He pointed to a microscope on the counter and indicated that Reiger should look through the eyeglass. Reiger said, "Now you sound like a witch. Goat's foot!"

"I tell ya, those Mississippi summer visits to your grandparents came in handy," Yu said as Reiger who was looking at microscopic fat worm-like creatures swimming on the slide.

"My grandma's garden had all kinds of herbs and vegetables and mushrooms," Reiger said as he was trying to figure out what he was looking at exactly. "She always said to stay away from gills on land, and any plant with a skirt. Or sometimes she called it the sack of a mushroom that could be buried in the ground. Those were the dangerous mushrooms that you might mistake for the edible kind." Reiger looked up from the swimming creatures. "I don't even like mushrooms."

"Tell me!" Yu paused and pointed to the slide "That's the culprit. Did your grandmother get you to eat mushrooms like my mother? If I made a fuss, my mother pulls out the famine card from the old country." Yu made a face. "You know, starving children in China."

"Of course. Only in my grandmother's scenario, the starving children were in Africa. Speaking of the old country, Mrs. Amy Davenport Emerson told me she hates San Francisco. She's from old money. East coast. The west isn't to her taste. Interesting woman. She never attended any of the fundraisers.

According to her, part of David's job was to flirt with the donors' wives. Turns out he flirted with one of the biggest donors, the grocery magnate Mary Fairchild, and she flirted back. But the affair that really got to her was with one of her own friends, a Gretchen Stenholm. Mrs. Davenport Emerson didn't seem to like her husband very much."

"There you have it: motive. And marriage." Yu picked up the test tube. "I like having a girlfriend. Keeps me out of the courthouse. Hey, wait a minute, what's with 'Davenport Emerson'?"

"That's how I know she's from old money." Reiger smiled. "It's the patrician way to use a family name as a middle name when you marry, if it's an important family. Say a Jacqueline Bouvier Kennedy, n'est-ce pas?"

"Oui! More power to Mrs. Davenport Emerson. I'm going to demand people say my name in the proper Chinese way, 'Yu, Edward.' Last name first."

Reiger's smiled broadened. "Well, Yu Edward, you like having a girlfriend because you live with your mother and she wouldn't approve of a Filipina girlfriend."

"You're too good, Detective." Yu grinned. "Now, to the matter at hand. Amanita bisporigera." Yu stopped swirling the test tube.

"Poison mushrooms. Destroying Angel—the deadly white. Just like we found in David's stomach and the vomit on his mouth and in the toilet."

AUTUMN DOERR

Yu set the test tube on a stand. Doesn't mean it was her mushrooms, though, right?"

"It did when I found mushroom paste in her garbage can." Reiger stood. "Just to confirm and dot i's and cross t's, the poison didn't kill him?"

"No. He got sick and expelled most of the poison." Yu wrote a note on his report. "The amatoxin is absorbed quickly but doesn't kick in until about 24 hours after ingestion."

"That explains why we didn't find any poison mushrooms at the office and Juanita confirmed she hadn't seen any containers."

"Who's Juanita, again?"

"The cleaning woman." Reiger tapped the side of his head.

"Oh, everyone's a suspect!"

Reiger chuckled. "No. It's a good idea to remember people's names. It makes them trust you and when they trust you—"

"When they trust you, they talk."

"I'll make a detective out of you yet."

"Stick with turning that Lexi girl into a detective. I'll stick to stomach contents and fatal wounds."

"That's a relief."

"So, what's really going on here?" Yu asked. "Why did David's wife want to make him sick with a potent poison that could have killed him?"

154

"First, access. The mushrooms are growing in their garden. The motive is as old as time. Revenge. David had lots of affairs, but this time, for her, he took it too far when it was the widow Stenholm. I confirmed with Gretchen—the hotel heiress who just so happens to rent an office from David Emerson at the institute—"

"Convenient."

"Very," Reiger said. "She admitted to the affair but said it was one time. She immediately regretted it and came clean to Amy. They're supposedly best buddies again. Here's the rub, the two widows are planning a world tour of her hotels."

Yu was astonished. "I guess they're assuming Amy won't serve time for attempted murder."

"Aren't you judge and jury? Let me at least arrest her first," Reiger said with a sigh more feigned than serious. "With the lawyer a Davenport Emerson can afford—"

Yu finished his thought. "Sometimes, crime does pay."

25

AN ARREST

Before leaving Dr. Yu's lab, Reiger had called Linda Corbin and sent her to the Emerson home to collect more evidence of the poisoning. Now in his own office, Reiger took his scarf from the coat rack and put it back on. It was almost as cold as the lab. The radiator had decided to stop working and he could see his breath.

As he typed his notes, the phone rang. He picked up.

"It's Linda. I can't believe Mrs. Emerson left the evidence in the kitchen sink." She was incredulous. "It was almost as if she wanted to be caught."

"Let me guess." Reiger sat back in his chair. "A dirty pot in the sink full of dishes?"

"It was." Linda was impressed. "How did you know?"

"It's the maid's day off and Mrs. Davenport Emerson doesn't do dishes." They laughed. "Did Stryker send his spies with you to the house?"

"No. You asked for me. Thank you."

"Of course I did."

"Off the record, Sir, they don't listen to me and then take credit for my work."

"That sounds about right," said Reiger with a sigh. They hung up, he had the arrest warrant ready and set the wheels in motion to have David's wife arrested for attempted murder.

26

THE FREEDOM INSTITUTE

The next morning at the Institute, Lexi stood in front of the bookshelves near her desk. It was time she understood what libertarians stood for and not just what people told her. What did they believe? She took down a book. The cover fell off in her hands.

The door opened and Reiger walked in. He saw Lexi with a cover in one hand and a block of wood in the other.

"What's going on?"

"It's not real." She said in disbelief. Reiger reached for another book. He read the title, *Capitalism: The Savior of the Masses.* Another fake. Each book on the shelf was a fake.

"I had no idea." Lexi was floored. She had gotten used to the crazy things going on around her. She had been making excuses and pretending that things were normal. Recovering, Lexi sat nervously at her desk waiting for him to say something about their last conversation. He sat down. They spoke at the same time. She said, "I'm so sorry," as he said, "Let's move on."

A wave of relief spread over her. It was time to wake up and get to the bottom of things, including answering the question: Who was Detective Reiger?

"Can I ask you something?"

"Maybe," he said, sensing a shift in her.

"You live in Oakland, right?" He nodded.

"Why aren't you a detective in Oakland?

"That's a complicated question."

"Is it that if you were there, you'd spend every minute looking for the person that hit your daughter?"

"Partly." He rubbed his mustache deep in thought. "It's also because it's my back yard."

Lexi let that sink in before admitting, "I get that. It's kind of why I left the bakery. To start fresh."

They were silent for a time. Lexi decided to keep asking until Reiger stopped answering. "How did you become a detective?"

"That's a long story."

Lexi waited, hoping Reiger would continue.

"I moved to Homicide during the great police strike of '75."

"I never heard of it."

"It's not something the city wants people to remember. The rank and file went on strike to get a raise but it's actually against the law for police or firemen to strike. You won't be surprised that the police are capable of flexing their muscles. In 1975, they just walked off the job."

"No!"

"Yes. The only people left to protect civilians were me and the other black officers, and a few managers who didn't disappear on leave. There were maybe 40 guys covering the entire city." Reiger stood to take off his leather jacket before settling back on the couch.

"Let me back up and give you a history lesson. Before the strike, black officers were given the worst calls and none of us were ever promoted. But the strike opened things up. For once, we could prove our worth. It turned out well for some of us for a while. Of course, Mayor Alioto caved, they got their pay and everything went back to the old way. But by then, I'd transferred to Homicide."

"I didn't live here then, but I can't believe I've never heard that story," Lexi said.

"You know, people forget that San Francisco is still the Wild West. The cops got drunk on the picket line. They shot out street lights and—I'm not saying they did it—but someone left a bomb outside the mayor's house."

Lexi was shocked. "I guess they followed the law until they disagreed with it."

Reiger sighed. "So here I am, a detective, and here you are, involved in another murder."

"I think 'involved' is a little strong." Lexi was pretending to be hurt. She told him she had asked Grey about the Ayn Rand book. It had not been a gift. "Grey didn't confront David because he could be vindictive and Peggy might have been punished."

"That's interesting. I knew Grey had lied to me. I got ahold of the Nevilles' bank records. Their house is heavily mortgaged. That's why it's surprising that Grey withdrew $1,200 in cash about six months ago."

"You think it was for the book for David?"

What he did not tell her was that there had also been a recent deposit for $2,000.

They sat in silence a moment.

Lexi pulled a worn copy of *Go Tell It On the Mountain* from her book-bag. "Remember recommending this book to me?" The cellophane on the cover was cloudy and dented.

"That's a good start." Reiger stood, pulled out a rumpled list from his pocket, and set it on the desk. Lexi read a few of the names: Toni Morrison, bell hooks and Eldridge Cleaver.

"The Bible?" She looked up and laughed. "Thank you. My education continues." She flattened the list, folded it carefully before putting it in her bag. "Don't you get down with all the killing you see?" She had wanted to ask him that for a long time. It finally felt like the right time.

Detective Reiger's answer surprised her. "I believe in God. To catch the bad guys, Lexi, everyone needs a reminder to be good once in a while. This place—" Reiger waved his hand indicating the office "—doesn't seem to be a good place. Covering up for criminal behavior is not you."

Lexi was speechless.

He continued. "Don't get cynical. That would mean you lose in life. You can't run away from pain. It won't bring Jerry back or your parents, and you'll end up alone. You could lose your moral compass if you're not careful. Think of the world as a mirror. What is it reflecting back to you? What do these people believe in? What do you believe in?"

"Well, at the bakery we believed in donuts." The attempt to lighten the mood fell flat. She knew he was right.

"How do you handle it?" Lexi could not meet his eyes. "The pain."

Reiger ran his finger over his mustache again. "God has a plan for us." He was so sure. "Jackie and I will see Jada again. It's not that it doesn't break our hearts every day that she's not here, but we know will be together in the end."

"I don't feel that in my heart."

"Someday you might."

"Did it occur to you that I'm traumatized?"

Reiger looked skeptical. "How about lazy?" Lexi's face reddened. She had been indulging her wounds and turning a blind eye. She made excuses for Julia and Jack. Even worse, she had been ignoring her life.

"Listen," Reiger said gently, "I don't mean to be hard on you but it seems to me—and I'm an observer of people—that a part of you doesn't want to let go of your pain. You can't use loss—even a loss like you've suffered—as an excuse to cut off your heart. Someday you might ask for help from a higher place outside yourself."

Jack suddenly appeared from down the hall. He held a Pall Mall in his hand, even though there was a "no smoking sign" posted behind her desk. Lexi pointed to the sign.

"Smoking keeps me company," he said with a smirk. "Have you seen Wicked?"

Lexi explained that Wicked was not in yet. Jack looked disappointed. He moved on, reminding her that she had promised to go dancing with him. She was about to blow him off as usual, but quickly decided it might be worth accepting if it led to finding more dirt on David. To Jack's surprise, she agreed.

"I'll pick you up at your apartment on Russian Hill."

"How do you know where I live?"

"Office files, my little friend. This isn't exactly Fort Knox." Delighted, Jack retreated back to his office and closed the door.

"You be careful there," Reiger said.

"I will. Promise." She asked, "Did you get the autopsy report?"

"We did. Juanita was right. David was poisoned by his wife."

"She killed him."

"She didn't. She's in jail waiting for a bail hearing. I don't believe she was trying to kill him. Just punish him. It wasn't poison that killed him, but I recommended an attempted murder charge to the DA's office. She could have killed him."

"She wanted to punish him for Mary?" Lexi said breathlessly.

"Gretchen Stenholm."

Lexi was floored. ""If she knew about Gretchen, why did she sit with her at the fundraiser? They had dinner together."

"According to Mrs. Davenport Emerson, David told her not to come to events because he was supposed to flirt with donors' wives."

"What a piece of work," she said, breathless with anger. "You know I hadn't thought of that. Friday was the first time Amy had come to any official event. She waited until he was dead. I wondered why she was even there? Was it because of Gretchen?"

"I should ask." Reiger stood. "Is Gretchen here?"

"Not yet. Oh my God! Could she have tried to poison Gretchen too?"

"I doubt it. David's poisoning wasn't that well thought-out. Don't you want to know how David died?"

Lexi almost fell out of her chair. "Yes!"

"The poison made him sick, but a blow to the head cracked his skull and knocked him unconscious. Then his organs shut down."

A shiver ran through her.

27

LIFE WITHOUT DAVID

Renée blew into the office, her feathered hair a perfect hair-sprayed helmet, her suit a shocking turquoise. She saw Reiger and stopped, dramatically. "Hello Detective."

"Just the woman I wanted to talk to."

"Well, I can tell you right now I don't know anything," Renée huffed.

"That may be the case. It's your institutional knowledge I'm interested in."

Flattered, Renée's shoulders relaxed as he escorted her to the conference room. The room was small. The space was crowded with a large oval table of dark polished wood surrounded by heavy plush chairs on casters. Once they had maneuvered two chairs away from the table, Renée poured them both a glass of water from a decanter on the table and sat down.

Reiger asked, "Where were you Wednesday night?"

"You get to the point don't you?"

"Wouldn't you?" replied Reiger.

Renée admitted that she would.

"Well, if you must know, I'll tell you. I was at home in bed."

Reiger didn't blink.

"Alone." She answered Reiger's stare. "My husband was away on business."

"Was there anyone who had a motive to kill David?"

Renée thought for a moment. She told him what he already knew. Mary and Gretchen. It wasn't much of a secret. "I could see why," she said. "He was a very handsome man."

Reiger waited for her to continue.

"Gretchen was a friend of Amy's. That might have been a breaking point."

"If she was a friend, does that mean she was a donor?" Reiger took a drink of water.

"Oh no. She's not a libertarian. She's a liberal."

"How do you know?"

"We have voter registration information. Let me be clear, it's all on the up and up. They're public record."

"Like Santa knows who's naughty or nice, you know who's a libertarian and who's not?" Reiger smiled to himself. Renée's face reddened.

"You and your husband seem to have been among David's biggest supporters. What did you think of his affairs?"

"It was his life to mess up. I'm not religious. It's true that I respected David. And what he does is his business, which, if you knew anything about libertarianism, Detective Reiger, you'd know that individual liberty is a tenet. We don't care what you do in your personal life."

Reiger was more amused than annoyed at her dismissive attitude.

He moved on. "What about the books?"

Renée shifted in her seat. "That's tricky for me. You see, I'll explain that I am the author liaison and that means I am the one who needs to justify setbacks and scheduling issues to our writers. It puts me in a very awkward position."

"How many books are outstanding this year?"

"Only two. Otherwise, we're on schedule. Two out of ten."

"So only two authors haven't been paid for books the Institute has contracted for?" he clarified.

"Correct." Renée drained her glass. "They would have been written eventually and now they absolutely will."

"Without David."

"I'll tell you one thing, I wouldn't have put it that way. This place *was* David. He built it with his own heart and soul. So to say 'without David' is—." She broke off and tried to compose herself before becoming emotional. "The Freedom Institute will go on but—let me tell you—it will be a shell of what it was without him."

28

WICKED SMITH

Later that day, Lexi checked off names of guests who had attended the fundraiser while Detective Reiger made calls in the conference room. Archie Greenway came in for a meeting with Renée. Lexi buzzed her. Renée came to the reception area, greeted Archie and they retreated into her office. Lexi wanted to know what they were discussing. She took a water glass from the kitchen and put it against the wall. She pressed her ear to the glass just as Reiger came into the reception area. He pointed to the glass.

Lexi cringed. "Well, I saw David do it once."

"Does it work?" Reiger sat on the couch.

"No." She set the glass on the desk and sat down in mock defeat. "It seemed to work for David.

"What's going on here?"

"Everything is different. It's like a free-for-all these days. Everyone is trying to get their pet projects going before the board figures out what to do next."

"Like what?" Reiger settled in.

"For one thing, Renée is pushing Peggy to finish Archie's book." Lexi leaned forward and lowered her voice. "And, Archie wants another book deal even though his first book hasn't been printed yet. I don't even think Peggy's started the first one. She told me she barely finished the slate of books due last year. It's already October. Expecting any books to be published this year is wishful thinking."

He pointed to the shelves of wood and paper. He said, "I've been through the ledger and Archie has not been paid for anything."

"That's weird." She paused. "Money could be a motive."

"Slow down, detective." Reiger was talking softly. "I've seen people kill for less but it seems like a stretch. Archie may need the money but why kill David? How would that get him paid? But, let's assume you're onto something. After motive comes opportunity."

"We can ask him." She was talking fast. "Let's ask him. He's here."

"I'll be the one to ask Archie questions. And when I need your help, I'll ask." His voice was kind, so Lexi relaxed.

"So, how about you?" Reiger asked. "What's your agenda? The pet project you want to get through before someone is appointed to run this place?"

"Agenda?" Lexi stopped to think. "Well, I do have something. I'm going to tell Julia she needs to stop drinking."

Reiger nodded with appreciation. "That's the kindest thing you could do for a friend."

The door to Renée's office opened and Archie walked into the reception area. Lexi introduced him to Detective Reiger who asked for a quiet place to talk. Lexi directed them to the conference room.

They sat down. Reiger asked, "How did you get involved with David Emerson?"

"I met David at the Hoover Institution at a conference at Stanford three years ago."

"When did David offer you a book contract?"

"Last year. I showed him papers I'd written for Hoover and he brought me in to meet Renée Samuelson. She does a good job navigating between David and the authors. I guess David could be prickly and didn't want to deal with writers. I didn't know him well but he was always good to me. I've heard stories from other writers, though."

"What kind of stories?" Reiger sat back.

"Well, I heard Ryan Callahan hasn't been paid for his book yet. Other writers are pissed that their books are ghost written. Peggy's a great writer, but nobody wants to take credit for someone else's work. You know what I mean?"

Reiger made a note. "Is this your first published book?"

"Kind of. My dissertation was on libertarian policies and how it will uplift the African American community. Put money in our pockets and not with big government. That's the book the Institute is publishing. It's basically written and just needs an editor."

"Why do you think it's taken so long?"

"Well, Renée—Miss Samuelson—explained that they have so many writers that want to publish under The Freedom Institute's banner that they're backed up. And she's been pushing for Peggy not to rewrite my entire book."

Just then, Lexi knocked at the door, opened it and stuck her head in, asking if they wanted coffee or tea for Reiger.

"None for me," Reiger said.

"I'll take coffee. Thank you." Archie looked relieved at the interruption. She shut the door as Reiger continued, "What's the name of the book, again?"

"You hadn't asked," Archie said. Reiger smiled. This kid was sharp.

Archie continued, "Libertarianism and the Prosperity of the African American Populace."

Reiger looked up from his notebook. "Catchy."
They laughed.

"Do you have a book contract?"

"I do."

Reiger decided to start with the premise that
Archie had been paid and see if he corrected
him. "Did you get paid in a lump sum or install-
ments?"

"Oh," Archie looked uncomfortable. "I've
been paid in one check. Have you talked with
Renée about this?"

"I'll verify it with her." Reiger had managed
to trip Archie up. He had closely examined both
Institute ledgers. One of the books recorded Archie as having been paid a large advance check,
but the other ledger recorded the exact amount
had gone toward "fundraising." That meant that
the funds had gone into David's secret account.
Reiger needed to know why Archie had lied, but
wanted to ask Renée first to find out if she, too,
would lie about the payment.

"Is there an issue?"

Archie smoothed his forehead with his hand.
"No issue. None at all."

"Can you dig up the check for me?" Reiger
watched as Archie shifted in his seat.

"Sure thing," Archie replied quickly.

"Now, where were you on Thursday, October
17th?"

"I was visiting my family in Baltimore. It's not a trip I normally take this time of year, but my grandfather's been ill and I wanted to check on him and my mom."

"Baltimore," Reiger mused.

Lexi knocked and opened the door. She set Archie's coffee down and closed the door behind her.

"I grew up there," Archie said proudly. "It's my home."

Reiger had made calls to get background on Archie. He said, "You were All American at the University in Maryland; graduated top of your class at Georgetown Prep."

"Detective," Archie nodded and tipped his cup to Reiger before taking a sip. "Go Terrapins."

Nodding back, Detective Reiger continued. "Let me ask you again. Have you been paid in full for the book?"

"I told you. I was." Archie seemed relieved to have something to fiddle with. He picked up his cup again, draining the lukewarm coffee.

Reiger sized up Archie, decided to let the money question slide for now and changed the subject. "I know how it is to be the only. The first. The only Black guy in the room. Do you trust these people?"

"I didn't trust David." Archie said, letting his guard down. "Man, he was slick. But I trust Renée. She's always been straight with me."

While Reiger was interviewing Archie, Wicked Smith bounced into the office. He was wearing a wide grin and had glassy eyes. Lexi handed him a message. "This guy hasn't received a book he ordered weeks ago."

Wicked's demeanor changed. He looked around as if to confirm they were alone and whispered, "Come with me."

Lexi followed him to the storage room. She had never been in there before. Wicked worked odd hours and often came in at night when he did not have a gig.

Unlocking the door, he continued to look over his shoulder to confirm that they were alone.

"Why are you acting like we're doing something wrong?"

He shushed her and turned on the lights. It was a small narrow room. Stacks of books lined shelves along one wall. A postage machine sat on a crowded counter. They squeezed into the tiny space. The fluorescent lighting cast a bluish glow. A stack of books in various stages of mailing crammed the counter. Lexi picked up a book on the outgoing pile titled *Radical Liberty*.

"These are old books."

He said, "That's the thing. There are no new books. I'm serious, mate."

"What?" Lexi stared at Wicked. "But what about all the books in the newsletter?"

"Like everyone else who gets that rag, you don't read it. Those are the same books from last year."

She thought of the wooden "books" in the reception area. They must have been books from years before she had started, books that were never written or published.

There was a noise in the hall. Wicked put his finger to his lips and turned off the light. "What are you doing?" Lexi whispered. She started to feel unsafe. "Let me out of here."

"Shh," Wicked said, turning the lights back on. "They're gone." He was standing with his ear to the door.

"Let's get out of here." Lexi started to open the door. Wicked stopped her. "Nobody knows this except Peggy and me."

"And David when he was alive," Lexi said. She pushed past him, opened the door and walked out.

Lexi sat at her desk nervously shuffling papers, waiting for Reiger to finish his interview with Archie. Wicked had ducked out before she could ask him more questions.

The conference room door opened and Reiger and Archie came out. Archie handed Lexi the empty cup and thanked her before he left.

Lexi quietly told Reiger about Wicked and the missing books.

"It's October." Lexi was incredulous. "We had a launch party in August for three new books."

Not wanting to involve Lexi any further in the investigation or put her in any danger, Reiger did not tell her about the ledgers.

29

DISCO JACK

Lexi had not told Cosmo on their nightly call about going out with Jack. It didn't make much sense to her why she was going, so why answer a lot of awkward questions? Somewhere in the back of her mind she remembered Reiger's advice to check her moral compass.

As promised, Jack picked her up at 9:00 p.m. She had wanted to make it an early evening but that was not how Jack rolled. Saxman had darted out of her apartment into the hall.

"Saxman!" she said, her voice stern. She scooped her up before she could reach the front door.

"What is that?" Jack asked, eyeing the cat suspiciously.

"What's what? My cat?" Lexi asked amused.

"No. That name?"

Lexi tossed Saxman gently into her apartment, grabbed her purse from a bench in the hall and closed the door before Jack could get a good look.

"Saxman Bite. It's a—"

"Stupid name!" Jack chuckled as he walked out the front door and waited for Lexi to follow.

"No. It's not." Lexi was indignant. "It's the name of a totem pole park in Ketchikan where I grew up. It's a Haida name. I don't think they would agree that it's stupid." She moved through the door as Jack let go and raced down the stairs to his car. He turned and said, "It's still a stupid name for a cat."

His black Beamer reeked of pot and she choked on the smoke. He handed her a joint. She was nervous but she took a hit. The only other time she had tried pot she had not enjoyed it. Her heart started to beat fast as Jack sped down Union Street toward North Beach.

It was cold and the lining in her men's tweed jacket was thin. She wore nylons under her short skirt and ankle boots. She wished that she had picked the turtleneck over the silk blouse, until she started to sweat and feel strange.

She turned to Jack. "Did you put drugs in my drugs?"

"Are you high?" Jack answered. They started to laugh and continued until Lexi started to choke. By the time she caught her breath, they were parked outside an alley on Vallejo Street. Disco pounded from Margrave Place. A crowd spilled into the alley from the club as the smell of piss ping-ponged around. She was very high.

In the tiny club, a disco ball swirled sending prism light into every corner. Everything seemed sharp and in deep relief. Lexi and Jack danced across the floor to the bar. "Excuse me," Lexi said pushing her way through patrons as they gave her nasty looks. Jack yelled to the bartender and squeezed Lexi in beside him. The bartender, displaying his chiseled physique in a wife-beater and tight jeans, set two drinks on the bar. Trying to seem more worldly than she felt, Lexi did not ask what it was before taking a swig.

"Eww! What is that?" She pointed to the glass, yelling over the noise in the bar.

Jack understood and answered, "A fuzzy navel. "Peach schnapps, OJ and vodka."

The second sip was not as bad. Jack chugged his, slammed the glass on the bar and dragged Lexi to the dance floor. The song "Hot Stuff" turned into "Rapper's Delight" then morphed into "When Doves Cry." She was hot and sweaty and ready to go home. She walked off the floor and maneuvered her way to the bar. Her drink was long gone but the bartender put a fresh glass in front of her. She marveled at his efficiency and lifted the glass to toast him. He grinned before moving down the bar to the next customer.

Jack had followed her. He pressed up against her. She handed him the remainder of her drink and yelled over the music.

"You know everything that happens at the office, right?"

"Only as ammunition, my dear. My motive is cash." Jack smiled for the first time tonight. "I'm taking bets on who killed David." He drained the glass. "My money is on the wife."

"Mrs. Emerson?" Lexi was surprised. "I don't see her having the strength to bash David over the head. He would have stopped her."

"Hell hath no fury." Jack leaned closer, his boozy breath made her nauseated. "She found out about David and Mary. Case closed."

"How do you know what Mrs. Emerson knew?"

"I have eyes and ears. You know Amy came in once when Mary was sitting in David's chair and David's nowhere to be seen. You must have been helping Peggy with galleys or hanging out with Julia because it was a scene. Mary was cool as a cucumber! And there was little 'ol Amy white as marble! I have to hand it to her. She kept her cool and stuck out her hand. Mary shook it like she was touching a snake."

Lexi had to laugh. "Cucumbers, snakes, marble. How does that prove anything? Hey, where were you?"

"I was watching from the door. I was right behind Amy. I expected Mary to act like the queen bee." He snorted.

"Slow down." Lexi's hands formed a "T" for time-out.

"Okay." Jack took a breath. "Mary gives us the most money of all donors except the Brothers Grimm—" Jack was exasperated by Lexi's perplexed expression. He explained, "The Clark Brothers. So, Mary gets to do whatever she wants. Amy knows that, but she could tell in that second with Mary sitting in David's chair like it was a throne that David was sleeping with her. Only she couldn't kick Mary to the curb like she wanted. And I know that because Amy and I are friends and she told me."

"You're 'friends' with David's wife?"

He tapped the side of his nose with his index finger. "She sometimes needs a mother's helper."

"What!" Lexi couldn't help but laugh at the absurdity of it. "There's no way Amy Emerson does coke!"

"Believe what you want."

"Okay. Whatever you say. So, Mrs. Emerson was all sugar and spice to Mary's face but behind her back, she had daggers out." Lexi was imitating how Jack talked. She felt bad. It was mean. David didn't treat his wife with respect so teasing about her felt wrong. Jack snorted a laugh. "Exactly! And if you mean by 'sugar,' Amy's coke habit, now I know you're getting the picture."

He poured white powder onto the back of his hand, took a rolled-up bill from his pocket and snorted it right there. Lexi looked at the crowd around them but nobody seemed to notice or care.

He yelled, "You're pretty chummy with that cop."

She changed the subject. "Were you blackmailing David?"

"Ha!" His head shot up. "That cheap bastard wouldn't pay anyone to keep quiet. If I threatened him with, say, telling his wife about Mary, he would have said point blank to go ahead and tell her. He was brutal, especially to those he supposedly loved."

"Did he find out you were spying for the Reed Foundation?"

"Touché!" he said as he grabbed her and flung her into the middle of the dance floor. She bumped hard into a muscular man with a shiny bald head. He shoved back sending Lexi into another dancer. Punches were thrown. Lexi took blows from every side and was pushed into the door frame before spilling outside. She was the first domino to fall, careening into a group of smokers. They collapsed into a pile.

She tried to right herself as a jab to her rib sent her back to the ground. She looked up. It was Jack. He leaned down and said, "Don't play innocent with me. Forget what I told you or else." If Lexi had been sleepwalking since Jerry's death, she was wide awake now.

She managed to get on all fours and crawl away. Once on Vallejo Street, she sat with her back against a wall and caught her breath. The cold air sobered her and shock kept her from feeling the pain in her ribs and knee. Her nylons were ripped and the scab from her roller skating fall had ripped off. The exposed wound started to bleed.

Jack was nowhere in sight. Her ribs ached as she stood and limped to Columbus Avenue. A cab drove up as she swayed on the curb. By some miracle, her purse was still slung over her shoulder.

She threw some cash at the driver, gave her address and thanked him profusely for picking her up. It was a short trip to her apartment. She managed to get inside. Saxman was circling her feet and she barely made it to the futon in the living room before tripping. She lay there, her head spinning. Everything hurt. Saxman was now circling her head, purring. The sound reverberated in Lexi's ears.

After what seemed like hours, she got up and ran a bath. She stripped off her clothes and sprawled on the bathroom floor wrapped in a robe. Saxman climbed on her stomach. Lexi winced as the cat pressed against her ribs but she didn't move. Her beloved cat was just what she needed.

30

WEDNESDAY AT THE FORTUNE COOKIE FACTORY

The light from the bay window streamed into the studio apartment window. Lexi woke with a vicious headache and pain filled her body. Lexi took a cold shower and tried to rinse away the terrible night. She wore a long-sleeved shirt to cover the bruises on her arms. She washed down a few pain pills with her tea and felt grateful there were no marks on her face. She didn't want to tell her friends about the brawl. They were her chosen family and she didn't want to upset them.

She was grateful that the office was closed for the board meeting, but almost sorry she had agreed to meet her bakery friends. She had accepted an invitation to visit a fortune cookie

187

factory in Chinatown. Ben had explained during their last poker night that McCracken's had filled a huge order for cakes shaped like fortune cookies for a gala honoring the Chinese opera.

"I don't know why they don't just order huge fortune cookies!" Ben had huffed.

Minh had called him out, "You love the challenge."

Ben, Stella, Henry and Tiny Timm met Lexi at the corner of Jackson Street and Ross Alley. The painkillers were taking a long time to kick in. Her head was pounding. She winced as she pulled her overcoat tight against the cold October air.

Ben caught her eye, but said nothing.

Stella looked at the sky dotted with clouds that stretched like a quilt above them. She said, "Look at those buttermilk skies."

Henry looked up and, even though his eyes were not what they used to be, he knew what buttermilk skies looked like. "That's Hoagy Carmichael."

"You got it in one." Stella socked Henry in the arm. She only came up to Henry's shoulder but her tiny arm packed a punch.

They sang, "Ol' buttermilk sky, I'm-a keeping my eye peeled on you." Looking up, Lexi's mouth went slack. She shook her head.

"It's the name for those clouds," Stella croaked, pointing at what looked like cotton balls stretching across the sky. "Buttermilk skies."

"Where's your cute boyfriend?" Timm asked. "You break my heart with that boy."

"We have a schedule. I see him most weekends."

"Schedules aren't for boyfriends," Stella contributed. "They're for lovers having affairs on their spouses. Those people need plans."

"I can take you away from all this if you come viz me to ze Kasbah!" said Timm.

Ben growled, "Let's get this show on the road." He opened the door to a brick building just inside the alley. Henry, ever the tour guide, explained that the fortune cookie factory had been in operation for over 20 years.

As they entered, they marveled at the small, cluttered room. It was a narrow space. They watched Chinese women sitting on folded chairs in front of hot griddles. In front of them were slips of paper with fortunes scattered in a shallow dip in the table. Each woman took a fortune, held it between her fingers as she grabbed the flat hot cookie with bandaged fingers, folded the paper inside and pressed the edges. She then set the cookie onto a sheet shaped as a crescent to cool onto a baking sheet.

Behind the griddles where the cookies were baking, were stainless steel ovens. On top of the ovens sat statues, dolls and Chinese vases. There were red and gold banners high on the walls. Below were lanterns, colorful fans and shelves stuffed with fishnet bags full of oranges and what Lexi guessed were the women's lunches. There were coats stacked on a bench. There was a desk with old pictures, a calendar and a large clock.

Ben turned to Lexi and asked, "How is that nutty crunchy boyfriend of yours?"

Lexi was surprised. "What do you mean?"

"Mr. Hippie Hemp living-off-the-grid guy."

Stella joined in, "Don't knock it; hemp is the—"

"Oh, no!" Ben roared. "No lecture on the hemp revolution." His outbursts were typical for Ben and to his friends who knew his good nature, but the workers had lost their rhythm looking up at the disturbance.

They could not help but laugh even when their guide, a young humorless woman running back and forth from a tiny office to the floor, scowled.

"Is everything okay?" Stella asked. "Where is Cosmo?"

Lexi lied. "He had to work today."

"Trouble in paradise?" Henry leaned toward Lexi and waited for an answer.

"He's fine. We're fine." She didn't want to admit that she hadn't asked him to come.

Ben continued with his previous conversation. "Does he even wear deodorant?"

Lexi didn't want to admit that he didn't and it was not what she loved about him. She hoped the topic would move away from her relationship. Henry came to the rescue and changed the subject. "How's the investigation going?"

Ben said, "Tell us what's going on." She could tell he had noticed her movements were subdued because of the body blows she had received. She decided to tell them everything: that David had been using donor money as a piggybank. The authors who had been promised book contracts where being strung along. David had been having an affair with not just one of the biggest funders of the Institute but also with the heiress to a hotel fortune who happened to be a friend of David's wife.

By the time she described the cocaine-fueled fight at the disco with Jack who happened to be a spy for another libertarian organization, the group of friends had stopped looking at the cookie assembly line. They had formed a circle around Lexi.

"And Jack is so reckless. He doesn't care about anything. He just slams headfirst into everything. And he's a male slut. When I think that so many men have died from AIDS, and especially losing Dean, it makes me furious. The thoughtlessness. The selfishness." She finally fell silent.

Stella spoke first, "I understand why you're angry but, Lexi, check yourself. I know what drugs do to people, but you were right in there with that guy Jack doing drugs. We lost some of the best musicians to that shit. I'm not talking pot here, of course." Everyone nodded in acknowledgement. Pot was like food to Stella. She continued, "But cocaine is the devil. Right up there with smack. And don't even try and make this about Dean. He died because this heartless administration doesn't care about gay men."

Ben looked sternly at Lexi. "How long have you been using drugs?"

"I, I don't really." Lexi stammered. "That was the first time I had ever tried it.

"That's what the best drug addicts I came home from Nam with would say." He was angry. "My buddies came home alive but they were wounded in their heads. Their souls were broken. They ended up killing themselves with drugs they 'didn't really use.'"

"I'm sorry, Ben." Lexi felt truly chastised. "It's just that I can't figure out what's what. I don't want Detective Reiger to think Julia had anything to do with David's death. I was just trying to get information from Jack and got caught up in the moment. I don't care about drugs. I'll never do it again, promise."

Ben said, "That Jack is trouble and Julia is not your mother. She's not going to die and leave you."

The young lady in charge of tours scurried out of the office again to move them along. The next group of tourists was waiting. As they moved toward the exit, Henry hung back with Lexi. He tipped his hat back. His cloudy eyes focused on her.

"It seems to me that those aren't the nicest people you're working with." He squeezed her arm. She winced. "You don't have to do everything by yourself."

Lexi wanted to cry. She knew he was right. Reiger had made the same point. She had lost her way.

"I'm in way over my head," she said. Henry put his hand on her shoulder. "Don't feel bad. We're all looking for a family. We have one at the bakery now because of you. But this group you're involved with, they don't sound worth it." They reached the others in a small stock room stacked floor to ceiling with boxes. There was a small table with two bowls overflowing with sample fortune cookies.

Ben approached Lexi. "You be careful with those snakes in that viper's nest. Jerry's killers almost succeeded in eliminating you. I already saved your life once," Ben teased. "Don't make me do it again."

"Oh, that old saw," Stella said.

The tour guide stood at the table with the bowls of cookies and pointed like Vanna White on "Wheel of Fortune." She asked, "Do you want sexy or clean fortunes? These cookies are for restaurants." She pointed from one bowl to the other. "The others are for bachelor parties."

One by one, the friends took a cookie from the sexy pile.

31

THE LAUNDROMAT

Lexi had arranged to meet Cosmo at the laundromat at 3:00 p.m. after his shift was over. Every two weeks, they would do their laundry together and now it had become a ritual, though they usually started after Lexi got off work at 6:00 p.m. With the office closed, they were able to start earlier. She was often out of clean clothes because she hated doing laundry. This was a nice way to "kill two birds with one stone," as she put it the first time they had arrived with bulging duffle bags. Cosmo's reaction wasn't what Lexi had expected which was to laugh at her lame comment. Instead he had frowned and shook his head.

The laundromat was across the street from Timm's apartment in the Tenderloin District, an area of dilapidated pre-war buildings, pawn shops and strip clubs. During the fire marshal's

AUTUMN DOERR

investigation of Jerry's death, she and her friends
had come up with what turned out to be a hare-
brained idea to get information. The plan had
been to call the fire station where Jerry had
worked and ask for help at Timm's building.

They had disabled the elevator and Timm
couldn't navigate the steps to his 15th floor apartment because of his crutches. That part of the
plan had worked. Two firemen came and carried
Timm to his apartment. They told him that the
investigation had concluded and that Jerry had
been knocked unconscious by a falling beam
during a hotel fire. It had proved to be wrong, but
the caper had cemented the friendship between
Lexi and the bakery patrons.

Sometimes Lexi and Cosmo would stop in
and have tea with Stella while their laundry was
finishing since her apartment was nearby as well.
Stella was keen on Cosmo. They shared an affinity
for pot. He also liked her cranky nature and enjoyed her stories of singing jazz at the Purple Onion when Lenny Bruce, Gregory Corso and Jack
Kerouac might be in the audience.

Cosmo and Lexi's dirty clothes were mingled in a
large basket on wheels at the washers. After load-
ing the laundry into two machines, Lexi put quar-
ters in the slot and started the washers. Cosmo
put his arm around her and asked, "Tell me about

that totem place? The one your cat's named after."

"Again?" Lexi gave Cosmo a playful bump with her shoulder. "Don't romanticize Alaska. I get that all the time especially from guys. It's a hard place to live. Nothing grows because it's all volcanic mountains so they import everything and it's expensive to live there." Cosmo looked hurt so she relented. "Okay. I told you about the drinking and guns and the stuffed polar bears on Main Street."

"And the moose in the backyard," said Cosmo, his voice hopeful.

Lexi had to admire his tenacity. He was like a kid. "There are only 7,000 people in Ketchikan. It rains 136 inches a year. I didn't even know this stuff when I lived there. I had to look it up at the library." Cosmo lifted Lexi onto the top of the washing machine and looked expectantly for her to continue. She said, "Okay, the native Alaskans, the Haida and Tlingit Indians, used totem poles to identify their clan or family."

"Like a family crest?" Cosmo was grinning.

"Yeah. You would know who lived there by reading the carvings. Totem poles are a way to tell a story or record an event. I suppose it's like hieroglyphics in Egypt. Telling a story with images and symbols. So, there are animals that a family will be identified with and you'd see that animal carved. That's just what I read so I'm sure there's a lot I'm missing, especially from the Indians' point of view. It's fascinating. I didn't give totem poles much thought until you started asking me about them. I always loved them but they were just there, you know, like a piece of furniture."

"Go on." Cosmo said.

"You can't want to hear this again?" Lexi said. Cosmo was standing between Lexi's legs as she sat on the machine. She squeezed him and pulled him closer. "This is where it gets maddening. To natives, carving is sacred and my people and yours—white people—came and rounded up the totem poles and put them in a totem park. I don't know who named the place Saxman Bite." Lexi looked into Cosmo's eyes. "Happy?"

Cosmo was relentless. "More."

"And, the pipeline brought good jobs, we have an airport on Gravina Island and the fishing is still great."

"It's the third largest salmon capital in the world!" they said at the same time, cracking each other up.

As the washer continued its cycle, they returned to folding the pile of clothes from the dryer. Cosmo had taught Lexi how to smooth her jeans on a flat surface, folding them to create a natural crease using her hands as an iron. It worked best if the clothes were warm. The neatness of his clothes was one of the non-hippy things about Cosmo; that and his desire to become an EMT.

Once the "his" and "hers" piles were stacked and in their bags, they took a seat near the window. They watched as the last of the clothes tumbled inside the dryer.

Cosmo reached into his backpack. "Apple?"

"No thanks."

Sensing Lexi was done talking about her hometown, he changed the subject. "What's going on with the case? What about that lady who's always giving you a bad time—Lisa?" He took a bite of the apple. "Could she have knocked off your boss?"

"You mean Renée. I don't think she would have harmed a hair on David's head. She worshipped him."

"Maybe David came onto her or disappointed her in some other way? Those devoted types can turn."

"I don't trust any of them anymore. I thought I knew them."

Cosmo put his arm around her. She was still sore from the disco brawl but had told him that she had tripped over Saxman and taken a tumble.

"It has to be Jack. He had the most to lose. Reed would never hire him because he can't be trusted. They paid him to spy. David must have found out, confronted him and Jack killed him."

"But, what about that musician guy?"

"Wicked?" She laughed, dismissing the idea. She sensed that Cosmo was jealous of him.

"Lexi, I'm worried about you. It's been over a week and the killer's still out there."

Feeling defensive on Detective Reiger's behalf, Lexi said angrily, "That's right. It's only been a week. We have suspects coming out of our ears—"

"We?" asked Cosmo.

She corrected herself, "Detective Reiger." She took a breath. "And, you don't know anything about having someone you love who's been murdered."

Cosmo removed his arm. He turned to look at her straight on. "I'm sorry. I didn't mean to rile you or bag on your detective."

Lexi picked up her laundry bag and hugged it. It was still warm and felt comforting.

"Oh, babe, I am such a jerk. I know you have a history with Detective Reiger and—." She cut him off. "And he has my back which I can't say for you at this minute."

"Let's just drop it." He stood to throw the apple core in the trash. Walking back, he leaned down to kiss her. She tasted apple as she softened her lips to meet his.

32

THE FREEDOM INSTITUTE

At the office the following morning, there were no signs that the board meeting had taken place the day before. Juanita had cleared everything. The staff started trickling in beginning at 9:30 a.m., earlier than usual. First Renée, then Julia, followed by Gretchen. Wicked must have sneaked in when Lexi was in the bathroom. She could hear him rummaging in his office, the supply closet. Jack finally showed his face after 11:00.

By noon, there was still no Peggy. The only person who was concerned was Lexi. Everyone was beavering away in their offices waiting for news on the fate of the Institute. It was so quiet that Lexi was startled when the phone rang.

Detective Reiger said, "Lexi, I have some bad news."

"More bad news?"

"Grey Neville has been killed at his home and it wasn't an accident."

"What?" She stood as the entire staff seemed to materialize around her. Even Gretchen had come out of her office. "What–what happened? How?"

"He was struck with a statue," Reiger said.

"The lion," Lexi whispered. Lexi thought of the bookends in Grey's office.

"Listen," Reiger said. "I can't talk now. Just keep everyone there until I can make it in."

She told the small crowd gathered around her desk the news.

"Great," Jack's voice was dripping with sarcasm. "The office was closed yesterday so, again, we're suspects."

Julia folded her arms. Renée put her hand to her mouth. Wicked piped up with "Crikey" and was met with a chorus of "Shut up."

They were quiet for a moment before Renée said, "And one of us might be a killer." She leaned against the desk in a rare moment of vulnerability.

Jack seemed stunned and whispered under his breath. "I don't have an alibi."

33

ALIBIS

By the late afternoon, Detective Reiger had interviewed Gretchen, Wicked, Renée, Julia, Jack and Lexi. Wicked had been at a sound check at the Mabuhay Gardens, a Filipino restaurant and punk club at the stripper end of North Beach on Broadway.

Wicked told Reiger, "The Fab Mab has seen better days but so has punk, ya know what I'm sayin'? You should definitely come check us out, mate."

Gretchen had spent part of the day at a charity luncheon; Renée at a Giants game at Candlestick Park. Julia was having lunch with a friend at Liverpool Lil's near the Presidio. "Where generals take their mistresses," she had volunteered. Jack vamped a bit before saying he was at the Embarcadero watching a movie, though he couldn't remember which one. And Lexi was with Cosmo.

When Reiger had released the staff and Gretchen, all but Lexi left the office. Lexi made a pot of tea. She and Reiger sat in the conference room and talked about the case. It felt like the time they had shared drinks at the Golden Spike in North Beach after Jerry's memorial service.

Lexi asked, "Is Peggy alright?"

He told her he had already talked to Peggy. She was at home resting under heavy sedation. "She's devastated as you'd expect. She found Grey's body in his office." He anticipated Lexi's next question. "I can't tell you how he died but I can tell you that Amy is out on bail."

"Why would Amy kill Grey?"

"I don't know that she did. It's just an interesting coincidence. She has an alibi. According to Gretchen, she and Amy spent the day going over her legal strategy."

"How convenient," Lexi mused. "What time was Grey killed?"

"It's an estimate but sometime during the afternoon. There were books stolen, a jewelry box from their bedroom and I'm sure there were more things missing, but Peggy was in no condition to take inventory."

Lexi speculated. "Are you thinking it was a staged robbery? Otherwise, you wouldn't have interviewed the staff. You think it might be one of them, us? But why would someone kill Grey? And is it connected to David?" An uncomfortable thought crossed her mind. "Peggy's not a suspect, is she?"

"She has an alibi for the afternoon. She was meeting with Archie at Black Oak Books in north Berkeley."

Lexi was surprised. "I wonder why Peggy didn't tell me about the meeting with Archie?" Lexi looked at the calendar on her desk. "There's nothing here. Maybe because the office was closed she didn't think it mattered what she did."

Reiger poured more tea. "You're right that the robbery looked staged. There was a *Bay Book of Psalms* from 1640 that wasn't touched. A run-of-the-mill thief wouldn't bother stealing the books." Reiger continued puzzling it out as he talked. "It could be that Peggy staged a robbery to collect insurance money. If Grey wasn't expected to be at home, things could have gone south."

"That doesn't explain why the thieves took some books and not others." Lexi blew on her tea before taking a sip.

Reiger was thinking out loud. "Maybe the killer was after Peggy?"

Lexi stared at him. He continued, "You're the one who said it. The wheels are off this bus."

34

BAKERY DETECTIVES

Since the office had closed early, Lexi decided to head to the bakery in hopes that she would find a few of her friends. She was feeling unmoored over Grey's death. What possible motive could someone have to kill him?

McCracken's Bakery was exactly as she had left it a little over a year and a half before. The only thing that had changed was the neighborhood. Across the street, the blackened scar where the fire had destroyed a section of the Cathedral Hill Hotel was gone, rebuilt as if nothing had happened.

A shiver went down Lexi's spine as she turned her back on the hotel and entered McCracken's. The walls were the same faded Pepto-Bismol pink. The Styrofoam wedding cake under cloudy plexiglass was still missing a plastic rose.

The coffee pots steamed on the burners near the front door. There were a few customers sitting along the benches near the windows along Van Ness Avenue and Chester Alley. At a table near the donut cases sat Stella, Timm and Henry. Lexi didn't recognize the new girl behind the counter so she helped herself to a cup of coffee and joined her friends.

Timm looked at his watch. "You didn't get fired, did you?"

"No. Something much worse." They looked at her.

"There's been another murder. Grey Neville."

"Who the hell is that?" asked Stella.

Lexi explained that Grey was a rare book dealer who was connected to The Freedom Institute through his wife Peggy and that he would moonlight taking photographs of Institute events. She also told them the circumstances of Grey's murder.

"When was your boss killed?" Timm asked.

She counted up the days. "Eight days ago."

Henry said, "There must be a connection, don't you think?"

Lexi nodded.

Henry and Lexi repeated the detective's mantra in unison, "What do we know? What don't we know?"

They reviewed David's case so far. But as much as they tried, the group of amateur detectives couldn't figure out a link between David's death and Grey's. If Jack had a motive to kill David, why kill Grey? And down the list they went. Wicked had no motive they could identify. Julia might have had a motive to kill David but not Grey. Renée had no motive for either. Mrs. Emerson? Gretchen? They came up with nothing.

As she told them about the last time she had seen Grey, she remembered something. "Grey acted strange when he looked at one of the proof sheets. He pulled it out of the stack and turned it over like he didn't want me to see it. I didn't think much of it at the time. Maybe he saw something? Something to do with David's murder."

"Ma cherie, if it was something incriminating, how would anyone know about it?" asked Timm.

"Didn't you say Peggy had money trouble?" Henry asked Lexi before Stella interrupted. "You did! He was blackmailing the killer!" Stella said loud enough to elicit stares from other customers.

Henry said to Stella, "That's not bad." He turned to Lexi. "Are the photos still around? Maybe you could take another look."

Lexi remembered something Renée had said and repeated it. "You can tell a lot from a photograph." She turned to the group and said, "I'm going to Grey's celebration of life at their house. I can look around while I'm there." Everyone agreed it was a terrible and possibly dangerous plan. They also knew she would do it anyway.

That night, Lexi stared at Saxman lying on the kitchen table as she waited for her scheduled 6:00 p.m. call with Cosmo. Saxman's tail rose and fell hypnotically. She peeled herself off the table, stretched her long body and jumped onto the floor. The fact that Lexi let her cat on the table disturbed Cosmo. It was another reason he preferred his boat to her apartment.

When the phone finally rang, Lexi jumped and Saxman looked up from the china saucer where she had been eating dinner.

"Sorry, Sax."

Lexi told Cosmo about Grey.

"Do you want me to come over?" She knew she should answer yes, but she wanted to be alone. "No, honey, it's okay. I'm exhausted. My grandparents are calling soon and you know they can wear me out. I really appreciate the offer though."

"If you're sure." They hung up. She lit one of her last two emergency cigarettes and heated a pan of old coffee on the stove. The phone rang again.

"Hi Grandma!" Lexi feigned excitement.

35

DAYS GO BY

The following week dragged on. Everyone was marking time knowing that The Freedom Institute Board of Directors would meet sometime during the week to decide their fate.

They had called a meeting in the conference room on Tuesday afternoon but it was mostly a pretense. Even Wicked had attended. They sat around the table and swiveled in their chairs like children.

Juanita served sandwiches, soft drinks and to everyone's surprise, a bottle of wine.

"Not that I don't love it, but what's with the wine, Juanita?" asked Jack.

"You libertines love to drink," she said.

"Libertarians," Renée said very slowly. Juanita winked at Lexi who giggled.

Jack halfheartedly asked where the negatives from the fundraiser ended up. "We need to order some prints for the next newsletter," he pointed out, as gently as possible. When Peggy said, "They must still be at my house," with sadness in her voice, Jack lost his enthusiasm for pretending to work. Renée seemed genuinely upset at the lack of focus and the issue of the negatives had been the last straw.

Wicked said, "Calm the 'H' down, man."

That would be the last meeting Wicked would attend.

Renée left the room in a huff, breaking up the meeting.

On Friday, the board met with the staff. They asked a lot of questions that were hard to answer since no one seemed to know the status of anything.

The board had announced that the new president was a man nobody had heard of. It seemed bizarre considering the libertarian world was small and known to cannibalize from within when it came to talent. The board's decision was that instead of closing early on Halloween, the offices would be closed for the entire day out of respect for Peggy who—suddenly and appropriately—became the most valued employee.

Grey's celebration of life was planned for the day before Halloween. Since Halloween was the city's most celebrated event, it seemed the right call. There was also gossip that the new president wanted to go through the files without interruption. Jack had speculated that the board assumed the files would be more accurate than what the staff would say about the status of projects. "That's until they see what I've done with my files" he said with a mysterious glint in his eye.

Lexi hadn't heard from Detective Reiger since he had called to tell her that his boss had assigned him two more cases. The release of Amy Davenport Emerson until sentencing had fueled speculation in the office that she might have killed Grey, though no theories of motive followed. Lexi told them Gretchen had given Amy an alibi. The consensus was that there must be something going on between those two. Lexi didn't tell them her idea that Grey might have found something to blackmail the killer with.

She had looked at all the proof sheets she could find in Jack's office but nothing jumped out at her as out of the ordinary and she had started to doubt there was a connection.

"Grey's murder has nothing to do with David's," Julia said definitively. "Grey found someone robbing his house and they killed him. Find the thieves, find the murderers." Even Gretchen had gathered in the reception area to gossip, though she was mum about Amy.

"Everyone has an alibi for David's death," Jack said. Lexi thought he was a man who liked an alibi and seemed to need them more than your average person.

"I'll tell you one thing," said Renée. "I've never trusted that punk rock stock boy."

"I kind of like him," Gretchen said, winking at Lexi. "This office can be dull."

"Apart from murder," Lexi reminded her. Jack, Gretchen, Julia and Renée drifted back to their offices leaving Lexi alone.

36

GREY NEVILLE'S CELEBRATION
OF LIFE

Lexi had asked Cosmo to come to the Nevilles' home for what she had started calling "the big kiss-off." Lexi had been asked by the board to come in early and show them where the files were. Cosmo had a key to her place and would let himself in after his shift. Once Lexi got home and changed, he would drive them to Berkeley. There would be no church service. Peggy told Lexi once that Grey had teased her that the only religion for a libertarian was the worship of money. Even though Grey rejected libertarianism, he hadn't set foot in a church since he was young and, despite his family's objections, there would be no religious service.

Lexi arrived home to find Cosmo sitting with Saxman purring loudly in his lap. She changed into a black dress, tights and boots. They left the apartment and drove to north Berkeley.

It was dusk when Cosmo parked on a broad tree-lined street. He and Lexi walked hand in hand to the Nevilles' house. Just before reaching the house, he stopped and asked Lexi if she was all right. She reassured him and squeezed his hand. They walked up the stairs to the porch. There was a heavy oak door with long, stained glass windows. Lexi could see there was a big group inside. Before they had a chance to ring the bell, Peggy opened the door.

"Lexi!" Peggy grabbed her and squeezed for a long moment. Once she was released, Lexi introduced her to Cosmo. Peggy gave him the same hug, as if she were clinging on for dear life.

Once inside, Lexi nodded to Julia who was holding a large glass of white wine. Wicked, dressed in his usual ripped punk-rock uniform covered with safety-pins, was scarfing down mac and cheese overflowing on a soggy paper plate. Renée, in a jade green Anne Klein dress, a tailored style with massive shoulder pads, leafed through a book near the bookcase, training her eyes on Lexi as she walked in.

Grey's family was in the kitchen laughing and telling stories. Antique-book nerds, wearing sweater vests and outdated spectacles, perused the bookshelves and looked through the Nevilles' record collection. The Freedom Institute staff stuck together in one corner of the living room near Renée. Peggy had disappeared into the kitchen, soaking up the warmth of family.

After an hour listening to small talk and stories about Grey, Lexi excused herself from the group sitting on the couch, moving nonchalantly toward Grey's office. Cosmo caught her eye, but lucky for her, he was in the middle of a conversation with Peggy.

Grey's office was almost as she had remembered. It had been put back together more neatly. The lion head bookends were missing. There was a small pile of marked-up proof sheets spread out on the table in a jumble. At a glance, Lexi could tell that it was a fraction of what she had gone through with Grey. These had been the rejects, but someone else had gone through them. According to Peggy, the remainder of the proofs were at the Institute in Jack's office. The negatives must be somewhere here as well. She had already looked through these proof sheets and found nothing remarkable. There must be more.

She looked under photography magazines and flipped through picture books to find anything Grey might have hidden. She ran her hands above the books on the bookshelf and quietly opened the desk drawers. She found nothing but unopened bills, letters and invoices from bookstores.

She moved to the door and surveyed the room. She was about to give up when the headlights of a passing car flashed in the window. Her eyes caught something deep inside one of the cubbyholes of the desk. She was making her way across the room when she heard Renée and Peggy talking. They were moving down the hall, coming toward the office. Lexi moved fast. She reached in and found a few rolled-up proof sheets. Just as the two women walked into the office, Lexi slipped the pages into her open bookbag.

Peggy said, "What do you have there?"

"No—nothing." Lexi stammered, trying to think of something to say. "I was just looking in my bag for a tampon." She dug deeper into her bag rummaging for an imaginary feminine hygiene product.

"Honey, I have some on the back of the toilet if you need one."

"Thank you, Peggy. I really do." She squeezed past them and practically ran to the bathroom. Her heart was pounding. Once inside, she turned the lock, pressed her back to the door and took deep breaths to calm herself. After a moment, her breathing started to steady. Behind the toilet on a crowded shelf was a mug with a few tampons inside, with "Live Free Or Die" written across the front. Lexi managed to smile and took a tampon for good measure. She walked into the hall and returned to the party.

Finding Cosmo, she finished her wine and tucked her arm under his. "Let's get going. I still have to come up with a costume before tomorrow."

Cosmo wanted to drive her home and spend the night, but Lexi needed to look at the proof sheets and insisted he drop her at the BART station. She could feel something important percolating. There must have been a reason that Grey hid those contact sheets.

As they put on their coats in the doorway, Cosmo said, "Lexi I don't feel like it's a good idea for you to be alone." His voice was raised and people in the living room were glancing at them. She didn't want to argue so she dropped her voice. "I just need a night to recharge my batteries." Cosmo looked hurt. "I don't mean that you drain my batteries. I mean. Oh, I don't know what I mean. I'll see you tomorrow, okay?" She gave his arm a squeeze. "I'll take the ten o'clock ferry over in the morning."

"I don't like this." Reluctantly, he agreed. "I'll meet you at the dock in the morning." They left the house and were silent as they walked to the car. Cosmo drove her to the station. They kissed, then she was gone.

Back in her apartment, Lexi watered the plant Cosmo had given her. It was clearly dead, but she couldn't give up on it. She started to cry. She hadn't been moved by David's death, but Grey's was another matter. His death had brought up memories of Jerry. No matter how hard she had tried to move on, Jerry's life and the brief time they had had together was still with her, like the ache of missing her parents. Those earlier losses had been taking her down until she had met Cosmo.

Sitting at the kitchen table, Lexi looked through the proof sheets but saw nothing she hadn't seen before. Maybe she would see something in the morning when she was fresh. Disappointed, she set the pictures aside and remembered she still needed to come up with a Halloween costume.

Looking through her closet, Lexi pulled out a shiny silver dress from the '50s and decided to create a Christmas ornament costume. She poked a hole in the top of a black beret and dismantled a hanger. Threading the hanger hook through the hole, she wound the bottom wire inside the beret so it pulled close to her head like the fastener on an ornament. She wrapped the hanger hook in tinfoil to make it look more festive. She found a thick rubber band used to hold manuscript pages she had taken from her desk at work, along with a small supply of Post-its and pens. The rubber band plus the hanger would keep the beret on her head. Lexi looked up and realized it was past midnight, Halloween. She left the hat and the proof sheets on the table and flopped into bed.

She tossed and turned, finally drifting off to sleep. When her alarm went off at 6:30 a.m., it felt as if she had just closed her eyes. It was cold in the apartment. She put on her robe and slippers and turned on the wall heater in the hall.

Heating old coffee in a pan on the stove, she poured a mug and sat at the kitchen table. Saxman soon joined her, meowing for breakfast. Lexi obliged.

Wrapping her robe tightly round her, Lexi sat drinking coffee and trying to wake up as she read Herb Caen's column from yesterday's *Chronicle*. She had to leave by 8:30 a.m. to make the ferry. The late autumn sun was creeping its way through the window. Saxman stretched on the floor napping in the dim morning light. Lexi's cat was only four years younger than she and, at 17, had lost her hearing. That didn't stop Lexi from talking to her or cooing when they were nestled together.

Now that Lexi was more awake, she moved her new Christmas ornament hat and spread the contact sheets on the table. Each image had been beautifully composed but some had only the backs of important guests and others showed people eating or drinking, a no-no for newsletter shots. She didn't see anything unusual. Again, she thought of what Renée had said about what you can see in a photo. She searched the proofs one last time focusing on the backgrounds and the edges of the frame. Saxman woke, stood, stretched and walked toward the table, meowing.

"Well, Sax. I guess I was wrong. But why would Grey hide these pictures?"

Saxman crouched and jumped onto the table on top of the pile of photos, sending several pages to the floor.

Lexi laughed. "You're so right, Sax. This is bull." She bent, and was picking them up when something caught her eye in a photo of Amy and Gretchen sitting together. In the far corner almost out of focus, just in frame, was Renée, in a low-cut, full-length burgundy dress, facing Archie Greenway. Her fingers were tucked under the lapel of his tuxedo and their faces were very close together. A shiver went down Lexi's spine. It was the last picture on the sheet and that meant there would be another contact sheet that continued the series of shots.

She petted Saxman and said, "Oh my god."

Lexi considered not wearing the Halloween costume, but had worked half the night and into the morning to make it. She pulled on thick black tights and the dress, placed the beret on her head and fastened the rubber band under her chin. She pulled socks over her tights before lacing up her Doc Martens. Saxman, pleased with the early breakfast, had disappeared into the front room. Putting the page of contact prints in her purse, Lexi sat at the kitchen table nervously waiting for 8:30. Surely, there would be someone at Reiger's office by then. If only she could reach Cosmo to cancel.

At 8:30 on the nose, Lexi sat on a chair in the front room with the phone in her hand. She dialed the number on Detective Robert Reiger's business card. It rang a dozen times. She knew she would miss the ferry if she didn't leave now. She decided to try Reiger again from a phone booth near the terminal. The hat went on her head and the ornament costume was complete, She grabbing her book-bag and coat, gave Saxman a quick stroke on the head before closing the door behind her and running to catch her bus.

37

THE WITCHING HOUR

As she approached the ferry terminal, Lexi was on the alert, holding her book-bag snug at her side and watching for sudden movements nearby. She saw the ferry approach the dock and ran to a phone booth, digging for change and feeding the coins into the slot before dialing Reiger's number. The phone rang and rang. The clock on the ferry building read 9:30 a.m.

Finally, someone picked up. "SFPD." A female voice came on the line.

"Is Detective Robert Reiger there?"

"'fraid not. Can I take a message?"

"This is Lexi Fagan. It's really important that I talk to him but I'm at the ferry terminal on my way to Sausalito and won't be near a phone." Lexi watched as the ferry passengers lined up to exit the ship. There was a Gumby, a Luke Skywalker and a Spock. They started to descend the ramp. She would have to run to catch the boat.

"Is there a message in there somewhere?" asked the women on the line.

"Please tell him it was Renée. I have an image that proves it. I have it with me. Did you get that?" Without waiting for a reply, Lexi hung up and ran down the pier to the dock.

Once she had boarded the ferry, Lexi headed up to the deck. Though it was bitter cold she wanted to see the city from the bay. Catching her breath after running, she watched the dock slowly recede. The Ferry Building, Coit Tower, the buildings that made up the Embarcadero, the Transamerica Building all shrank as the ferry moved further away.

She turned to the north. The sky was clear as Alcatraz Island came into view with the Golden Gate Bridge shining in the west. Lexi could see sunlight gleaming off the windows of homes along the Sausalito cliffs. She enjoyed riding the ferry. It reminded her of the things she loved about Ketchikan, like the narrows at the base of Deer Mountain and Gravina Island across the water. She remembered watching the waves as they soaked the mussels and barnacles clinging to the pier, and she recalled the unmistakable smell of tar, motor oil and fish. Interrupting her reverie came the sound of children's voices in the distance. She couldn't tell where the sound was coming from or if they were laughing or screaming. It was unnerving.

October was her favorite month even though the 19th was the anniversary of her parents' death. She loved Halloween also because today would have been her mother's birthday. Now that she lived away from pitying eyes, she allowed herself to celebrate her mother. It made her feel grown up to make choices about her emotions and what she would and wouldn't focus on. October made her feel closer to her parents as she imagined them flying around the panhandle of Alaska, those twenty-some years ago.

As Lexi stood on the deck daydreaming, the wind cut through her. It was the coldest Halloween she could remember. The bay was rough. Waves slammed against the side of the ferry spraying the deck right next to her. A lone seagull careened overhead crying as a wad of gray and white descended, hitting Lexi on the shoulder.

"Oh no! One damn seagull and it hits me?" She was talking to no one in particular and laughed to herself. The other passenger on the deck, a man in a gray business suit, turned and took the steps down, safely inside. Lexi followed him inside to warm up. The lounge was nearly deserted. She picked a spot near the front of the boat and sat down adjusting her ornament hat that had slipped around her neck. She could hear people talking in the distance and assumed they were gathered near the concession counter at the stern. At least she thought it was the stern. She had been learning nautical terms to impress Cosmo and more often than not got them wrong. It seemed to make him happier than if she'd gotten them right.

The ferry from San Francisco to Sausalito was always empty this early on a weekday. The passengers flowed to the city to work. Today, there were a handful of people, mostly in costumes favoring characters from *Back to the Future*.

As if waking from a trance, she thought about how she shouldn't be here at all, but on her way to Detective Reiger's office. There was no one sitting in this part of the boat. Deciding that there was nothing she could do now, she relaxed and took out *Go Tell It On the Mountain* and started to read. She was startled by a voice she recognized that seemed to be coming from right next to her.

"In most cultures, if a bird defecates on you, it's considered good luck."

Lexi turned to see the long black robe, cape and pointy hat of a witch standing over her. She looked at Renée's twisted smile.

"Looks like your luck has run out." A hand from inside the cape swung at Lexi hitting her in the mouth.

"What the—" Lexi touched her face and stared at Renée. She felt stunned, like a bird smacking into a window, and shook her head to snap out of it. Recovering, Lexi swung her legs toward Renée and kicked as hard as she could. Renée staggered back and moaned. Lexi's ears were ringing. She was alone in this part of the ship except for a killer. As Renée gained her footing, Lexi got up and ran for the stairs, up to the deck to find someone for help, maybe the ferry's captain. Her movements were clumsy and she felt as if she were moving in slow motion. Her book-bag was slung over her shoulder and bounced off her back. It felt as if it weighed a ton.

When she reached the stairs she took them two at a time, grabbing the railing to steady herself. She could hear Renée right behind her. As she reached the top, a sharp wind cut through her and she pulled her jacket around her and grabbed her beret before it blew off her head and choked her. She swung her bag forward, wincing as it hit her ribs and shoved her hat into the bag.

"Alexandra." Why was it, Lexi thought, that nobody but killers and her grandparents called her Alexandra? Before Lexi could turn and confront her, a shove to Lexi's back sent her down a step, into the railing. She grabbed the top rung to stop her upper body from propelling her over the side. Renée was right behind her and grabbed her legs, attempting to hoist them over the top and finish the job.

To buy time, Lexi yelled, "Why did you kill David?"

Renée paused and said, "He was going to tell my husband about Archie. Clarks don't divorce. They destroy." Then she laughed.

A bone-chilling shiver ran through Lexi. It was like the feeling of walking through a spider's web. In that second, she realized that Renée had started to enjoy killing.

Detective Reiger stood at the entryway of the police station. It was unusually cold outside but the old radiators along the walls had turned the entry into a hot house. It was the opposite of his office. He had peeled off his scarf and gloves and was unbuttoning his leather jacket when the desk officer appeared.

"I have a message for you," she said.

Reiger nodded.

"A—" she looked at a pad of paper. "Something Fagan called and said to tell you: 'It is Renée.' And she has the photo to prove it."

Reiger waited for the rest, but was met with silence. "That's it? The whole message?"

The desk officer looked up and said, "She did say she was catching the ferry to Sausalito. She also said she won't be near a phone."

"What time did the call come in?"

She looked at the message pad. "Nine-thirty."

Reiger looked at his watch. It was 9:45 a.m. She might still be on the ferry. He thanked the officer and took the elevator to the third floor.

Once in his office, Detective Reiger tried to make sense of what he just heard. Why would Renée kill David? And where did Grey come into things? Lexi mentioned a photo. He thought back to the interview with Grey. He was the Institute's regular freelance photographer. Maybe he'd taken a photo of Renée doing . . . what? Whatever it was, Grey could have used it to blackmail her. The Nevilles had money trouble. That would explain the recent $2,000 cash deposit in Grey's account. It could also explain why Grey had been murdered.

Reiger needed to get ahold of the photograph in Lexi's possession. He also needed to search Renée's home. He found the Institute contact list. Page two listed everyone's home address. He scanned the page and found Renée Samuelson's address on Lyon Street. He picked up the phone and called Judge Rachel Steinman.

After the judge had issued a search warrant for Renée's apartment, Reiger called Linda Corbin from the forensics team. "Linda. I'm glad I caught you. Listen, I've got a search warrant for a Renée Samuelson's apartment in Hayes Valley. Can you pick it up from the desk officer and get over there to search the apartment? I'm looking for any old books, maybe a photograph and a map of Berkeley. And look for a Trannie." He paused for Linda to ask the inevitable. "It's an award shaped like the Transamerica Building. If there's blood on it, you get a brownie point. I'm looking for evidence that Renée killed David Emerson and that she broke into the Neville home and killed Grey." If Renée had destroyed the evidence, he would need to recover the photo or maybe even the negatives he hoped were in Lexi's possession. It was too soon to interview Renée. He would need solid evidence to bring her in.

He then rang the desk officer and asked her to consult a ferry schedule. The ferry had departed San Francisco at 10:00 a.m. and would dock in Sausalito half an hour later at 10:30 a.m. If he left immediately and used lights and sirens, he just might beat the boat to the terminal. If Lexi was not on it when he got there, he'd look for her at the dock. She had told him once that her boyfriend's houseboat was berthed at the poor man's dock across from Marin City. Grabbing his keys off the desk, he put on his coat and gloves and wrapped the scarf around him before leaving the stuffy building.

Lexi had a little traction as she hung over the side of the boat, holding the railing on the outside rung of the steps. She kicked with all her might to dislodge Renée. She must have taken her off balance because her legs were suddenly free. She used all of her strength to right herself. She stood on the deck and swung around with fists flailing. She landed a blow somewhere in the mass of cloak, making contact, and for a split second, she enjoyed the victory. Renée countered with a fist to Lexi's jaw. Her back now against the railing, Lexi grabbed the book-bag and swung it with what little strength she had left, knocking Renée to the ground with a thud.

Lexi watched as Renée rolled over and started to get up. Lexi's muscles ached and it was hard to catch her breath. As Renée lunged, she growled, "I'm going to show you—." Lexi cut her off by kicking as hard as she could into Renée's stomach throwing her back to the ground. The deck was damp and slippery. Lexi fell onto her knees.

As Renée started to get up, Lexi decided to stay down. She scooted toward the railing, swiveled her body and used her legs to push off the railing. Heaving herself backward, she slid across the distance between them, hoping to hit Renée's legs. She connected, knocking Renée back down.

Lexi rolled onto her side and sat up. She felt every muscle resist as she stood. Taking a big breath, she screamed for help but the wind swallowed her cries.

Renée stood and lurched forward. Lexi saw the fist and deflected it with her arm. Pain seared through her and she screamed again. Her book-bag was just out of reach and Renée was coming back for more. Throwing herself on top of the bag, Lexi was relieved she had landed on the part with clothes and not with books. Wrapping the bag in her arms as she continued to roll away from Renée, she was unable to stop herself from smashing into the feet of a bench. Searing pain in her back stopped when the first kick landed to her head.

Dazed, Lexi readied herself for the next blow. She grabbed Renée's leg as it slashed toward her, pulling Renée down. She yelped like a wounded dog.

It was hard to move, but Lexi knew she had to get up. She struggled, managed to get on all fours and scrambled from under the bench dragging her book-bag behind her.

"You witch!" Renée yelled.

"No, you're the witch!" Lexi screamed, looking back at Renée, now crumpled in a pile of black fabric, her pointy witch hat sprawled next to her on the ground, the strap still attached to her neck. By then a few passengers had heard the commotion and had surrounded Renée. Stunned and shaking, Lexi made her way to the upper deck.

Thinking of her mother, Lexi opened her book-bag, took out the crushed beret, and put it back on her head.

As the ferry pulled into the terminal, Detective Reiger could see Lexi hanging onto the railing of the deck. She had the beginnings of a black eye and her nose was beginning to crust with blood. She saw him and felt a sharp pain as she raised a hand to wave. Her jacket was open and her silver dress was ripped. Her beret was crushed, the wire hook hanging limply over her ear.

Before the ferry had reached the dock, Reiger had radioed for back-up and quickly called for an ambulance when he saw Lexi. Cosmo was also waiting.

The ferry docked. Lexi limped down the gangway. She hugged Cosmo and smiled weakly at Reiger. She explained that Renée was out cold on the lower deck and in need of medical attention. Reiger laughed, looking at the state of her bedraggled costume. He told her he had called an ambulance for Lexi, but they would use it for Renée. With a mixture of relief and adrenaline, Lexi knew she had to tell Reiger what had happened immediately and agreed.

Lexi's words rushing out, she asked Cosmo if she could come to the houseboat after she had gotten cleaned up and had debriefed Reiger. The Sausalito police arrived and escorted the ambulance that took Renée to the hospital.

Cosmo insisted he take Lexi straight to the emergency room.

Reiger said, "I'll take her to the E.R." Reiger gave Cosmo a reassuring pat on the back. "Don't worry. I'll take good care of her." He felt sorry for the guy. Lexi wasn't the easiest girl to look after.

Feeling dismissed even with Lexi's assurance, Cosmo walked to his car, leaving Lexi and Reiger on the dock.

Reiger drove Lexi to the emergency room at a hospital in Sausalito. He had to flash his badge to get her to the front of the line. "It's Halloween," said the nurse dressed as a sexy nurse. She apologized to the three people sitting in the waiting room also wearing costumes as she ushered Lexi into a small examination room.

The doctor told Lexi there wasn't much he could do about the bruised ribs. The nurse wrapped her broken finger, cleaned her bloody face and released her with a few painkillers. An hour later, she and Detective Reiger were sitting at the Taste of Rome.

38

HALLOWEEN

Savoring the best latte she had ever tasted, Lexi felt the adrenaline drain from her body. Even with a stuffed-up nose, she could smell the rich coffee and cigarettes in the cafe. Reiger observed the costumes of patrons and people on the sidewalk outside. He told Lexi that his wife had been right when she guessed the costumes this year. There were Doc Browns, a Princess Leia and a man with a powdered white face, beard and long eyelashes wearing a nun's habits. They watched as a Doc Brown in a shaggy white wig asked what he was dressed as and he said, "Dahrling, I'm a Mother Superior with the Sisters of Perpetual Indulgence! Bring me a coffee or I'll wrap your knuckles, young man." Everyone laughed as the nun took out a long ruler from under her robes.

"This is one reason why I love Halloween," Lexi confessed. She pointed to a couple sitting at a table in the corner. "There's a Darth Vader and a throw-back to the '70s." Reiger stared at the scary looking young woman wearing a dirty night-shirt.

"Linda Blair from 'The Exorcist,'" Lexi explained.

Reiger nodded. "Let's get down to business." Lexi opened her book-bag. It was ripped and dirty, but to Lexi's surprise, still held its contents. She pulled out the contact sheet and handed it to Reiger. "It's the last shot on the roll." He held the paper close to his eyes and was silent for a moment. "I see it. Renée and Archie. How did you put it together from her touching his lapel? And what made you think there were more incriminating photographs in Grey's office?"

"It was my bakery friends and I who figured it out," Lexi said. "When Grey and I were marking up the proof sheets, he must have seen something in one of the pictures. If Renée's husband found out about the affair, it was over. Her influence. Her power, gone. She admitted it while trying to throw me off the ferry." She explained that Grey had pretended he had made a mistake on an important photograph of a donor. Since she didn't know Grey very well, she took it at face value. Looking back, she realized that Grey didn't make mistakes like that. "He snatched the proof sheets away and covered them so I wouldn't see. It wasn't until I found this shot that I realized that the next contact sheet might have been the two sneaking a kiss."

Reiger said. "There was also the truth about the books. Nothing was getting written. If that came out, Ralph would pull the plug. She had made promises to Archie and David turned her into a liar. She wanted it both ways, to keep Archie and Ralph. The Nevilles home was about to be taken over by the bank. Grey must have confronted Renée and threatened to expose her. And that's when he started to blackmail her."

Reiger continued, "I have a forensics team at Renée's home right now. I think we'll find the damning photo at the least. Obviously, we're hoping to find more than a picture. There were no fingerprints at the Nevilles' house. My theory is that Renée only meant to take the negatives and proof sheets. Grey came home and surprised her. She grabbed the closest heavy object and hit him in just the right spot. He went down after the first blow."

Lexi told him how Renée and Peggy had walked into Grey's office just as she found the hidden proofs. She left out the part about the tampon excuse.

"How did Renée know you would be on the ferry?"

"She overheard Cosmo and me arguing about him taking me home when we were leaving Peggy and Grey's house. He wanted to drive me, but I wanted to look at the proof sheets. I begged off and told him I'd meet him this morning at the dock in Sausalito. I'm sure she saw me stuff the proofs into my bag in Grey's office."

"What I don't get is where are the negatives?" Reiger looked at the proof sheet again. "The proofs mean nothing if the negatives are out there." Lexi recounted the conversation from the meeting at the office. This time she understood why Renée had gotten so upset when Peggy said they were somewhere in the house. "She killed Grey for nothing," Lexi said, her voice breaking.

They sat in silence for a while before Lexi asked, "When are you going to interrogate Renée?"

"Well, we don't interrogate people anymore." Reiger was amused. "Renée can cool her heels. Besides, she won't be released from the hospital for a while. You did a number on her." He smiled.

"What's going to happen to David's wife?"

"She'll be fine. She has a great lawyer from back east." Reiger looked at Lexi with concern. "The question is, what's going to happen to you?"

Lexi's eyes welled up. The shock was wearing off. "I don't know. I can't work for The Freedom Institute anymore. It's freedom from morals and, you were right, I was slipping. I feel as if I started to disappear from my own life."

Reiger raised an eyebrow. He didn't want to influence her, but was relieved she was leaving that group behind. "Back to the bakery?"

"No. I can only think about going forward." Lexi watched as a Madonna with spiked hair wearing a black halter-top under a leather jacket walked into the café. The long chains around her neck jangled as she approached the counter.

"First, I need to figure out what I'm doing with Cosmo."

"Take the deep breath of life." Reiger realized he was sounding like Dr. Yu and smiled. "And take your time to figure out what you want. This life is precious."

Darth Vader picked up a briefcase and he and Linda Blair stood, waved at the café owner and left for work.

39

COSMO

Lexi had Detective Reiger drop her at the pier. The painkillers were taking effect and she grunted as she climbed onto Cosmo's boat. She hugged him and laid down, almost instantly falling asleep. It was dark when she woke to the smell of food. Cosmo was making pancakes for dinner, her favorite. They drank coffee and ate, not talking for a long while.

Lexi said, "I can't— I can't—."

Cosmo put his hand over hers, "I know."

The boat rocked gently as they stood, hugging. They both began to cry.

"You know I can't compete with a ghost," Cosmo said.

"And I'm too damaged to let anyone help me and probably to let anyone love me."

"That's not true." He lifted her tear-streaked face. "You have a hard time and I get it. You've lost so much. But Lexi, you're not a victim. You're just feeling sorry for yourself. It's me you should be feeling sorry for." They both smiled.

She stepped to the stove to regain her composure and asked, "Do you want more coffee?"

"Sure."

Lexi poured the last of the pot and started clearing the dishes. "I'll try harder to let go of Jerry."

"You can't even leave a toothbrush," he sighed. "I see you check his badge inside your bag every time you pack up.

The smell of sour milk and motor oil made her feel sick. Cosmo stood and took the plates from Lexi's hand, setting them in the sink. "Do you want me to take you home?"

"I do." Lexi felt sadness pull her like an undertow. It was as if she couldn't hold onto anything. She thought about what Grey had said during their last visit, "Tragic, tragic love."

Back at home, Lexi sat in the kitchen. She stood and began to pace the floor before opening a drawer, taking the last emergency French cigarette from the pack, and threw it into the garbage. A minute later she dug it out. She lit it and took a long drag, the smoke burning her lungs.

She looked at her kitchen, empty save for Saxman curled in a ball napping. The old pan to heat water for her cone-and-filter coffee sat on the stove. The bare windows looked onto an alley and the apartment building next door. Cold air seeped through the crack at the top where the window was stuck. She loved the feel of the old table that she had rescued from the curb her first week in the apartment. She rubbed her hands along the wood, stained with old coffee rings and burn marks.

"Maybe we have a message, Sax?" she said, stubbing out her half-smoked cigarette. The answering machine was next to the wall on the table. There was a message from Detective Reiger. He had invited her to breakfast on Saturday, November 9th. She was flooded with a sense of relief. She picked up Saxman and hugged her. Her eye caught something green on the plant Cosmo had given her. There was a tiny green shoot on the stem.

The next day, Lexi was to meet Julia for lunch at the Iron Horse, a restaurant where they often went during the week. Julia always had a bowl of minestrone soup and Caesar salad with a strong smell of anchovy, washed down with two glasses of white wine.

Lexi's standard order was a BLT and a Coke. She thought of what she would say and how Julia might take it. Should she resign first and then confront Julia about her drinking? There was no scenario where things ended well, no matter in what order she said them.

Saxman wiggled out of her arms and jumped to the ground. "You're quite right, old girl. Best to wing it."

40

THE IRON HORSE

Lexi took the cable car to Union Square. She walked through the park to Maiden Lane on her way to the Iron Horse Restaurant. The Halloween decorations in the shop windows of Macy's and Neiman Marcus were already being taken down, replaced by tableaus of Thanksgiving. As she walked, Lexi noticed people were staring. It confused her until she realized she was still banged up from the fight. Her nose had a bandage from an abrasion and her eye was a deep yellow and purple. A cut on her lip broke open in the dry air, leaving dried blood on her mouth. She was grateful for the cool air that seemed to numb her wounds.

Inside the Iron Horse, the stained glass windows cast a vaguely religious glow over the room. Lexi walked toward their regular booth. The diamond shapes and primary colors of the glass reminded Lexi of a harlequin. Pictures of famous patrons lined the walls. The restaurant had once been a hot spot where Joe DiMaggio and Frank Sinatra rubbed shoulders with politicians like the current Speaker of the Assembly Willie Brown and the late mayor, George Moscone. It had been the place to be seen as they had climbed the political ladder in the '60s and '70s.

It was warm inside. She was already sweaty from her brisk walk and took off her coat and yanked off her scarf before sitting down. Julia arrived looking elegant as always. Her polished nails drew attention to her long fingers, showing off her expensive rings. She took one look at Lexi and said, "Oh my. You look like hell. You said you had been beaten, but that looks dreadful."

"I'll tell you all the gory details after we order." She pulled out an old Kleenex and dabbed her lip, which had started to bleed. "I'm starving."

They tucked into the booth. The waiter arrived and took their order. He couldn't take his eyes off Lexi's bruised face. Unsure what to do, she turned to Julia and asked the first question that came to mind, "Has this place ever been renovated?" Julia looked perplexed. The waiter answered, "It is how it was, darling, like your face will be one day."

They laughed. It broke the tension and though she was nervous about bringing up Julia's drinking, now was the time. She took a deep breath. The waiter brought wine for Julia and a Coke for Lexi. This time, he ignored her face.

To her surprise, Julia pulled a small sack from her purse and passed it to Lexi. She opened the bag and pulled out a pair of earrings with long strands of metallic mesh.

"They call these shoulder dusters." Julia said, pleased with the offering.

"You really shouldn't have." Lexi took out her studs and put them on. A man wearing a white suit walked by the table and stopped. "Those look good, little lady," he said. As he walked away Julia said, "He's wearing what we used to call the 'Full Cleveland'—white pants, white belt and white suit jacket." They laughed. The waiter brought their lunches and Julia's second glass of wine.

Lexi stared at her food. "I wouldn't say this to you unless I cared. I don't want to hurt your feelings." The words came rushing out.

"What is it? Is everything okay?"

Lexi looked up and blurted, ""I think you have a drinking problem."

Julia paused for a split second before taking a large drink of wine. "Has it gotten that bad?" Relief washed over Lexi.

They talked about all the ways Julia had been slipping.

"Where are the books?" Lexi asked.

"Which books?" Julia looked as if she'd been struck.

Lexi continued, "The books that donors pay the Institute to publish. How could David keep it up? Somebody was going to notice there were no new books being printed."

"They did notice." Julia drained her glass and looked for the waiter.

"Things got out of hand when the board chairman asked to audit the books." She caught the waiter's eye and raised her empty glass. "David was about to throw me under the bus and accuse me of embezzling since, on his orders, I was keeping two sets of books." Lexi hated to admit to herself that this could have been a motive. At least it hadn't led to murder.

The waiter came with a full glass of Chardonnay. "I promise I'll clean up my act, just not today." She gave Lexi a wan smile. The waiter started to turn to leave when Lexi said, "I'll have what she's having." She needed to build up the courage to tackle the next topic. The waiter said, "Honey with that face, this one'll be on the house." His southern accent, subtle when they first arrived, had turned thick. Lexi thanked him warmly before he retreated to the bar to fetch her wine.

Julia said, "We don't have to go to work today so what the hell? Right?"

The waiter brought the wine. They continued to eat as Lexi described the beating she'd gotten from Renée on the ferry.

"I hope she looks worse than you."

"She does!" said Lexi, already feeling tipsy.

They laughed that Renée had dressed up as a witch. Lexi went on to describe how Detective Reiger had gotten Lexi's message, met the ferry and arrested Renée before the ambulance took her away. Feeling the wine loosen her tongue, Lexi went on to tell Julia about the breakup with Cosmo. Julia had been married and divorced a few times and understood heartbreak and disappointment. Finally, the conversation waned. The time had come.

Lexi said, "There's one more thing."

Julia waited for Lexi to continue. "I need to leave the Institute."

Julia's shoulders slumped. "Oh my. I was afraid of that." She raised her glass. "Listen, I was right to hire you and it's right for you to move on. You know I appreciate how much you took care of me." After a beat she said, "You really aired out my office?"

"Every day." Lexi raised her glass. "I'd do it again except I don't want you to get hurt or fired or lose any more of your life to booze." They clinked glasses.

41

It was a golden day. Oakland seemed to gleam from a recent rain. Lexi breathed in the fall air, cool and damp. The early morning sun slanted softly through the trees as she walked to Jackie and Robert's home. She reached the yard and nervously checked her book-bag for the book Peggy had given her as a gift for Jackie.

The yard had large oaks with shorter bushes growing below. She walked up the stairs to the wide porch. Its large pillars looked freshly painted. Shortly after hearing the doorbell, Jackie opened the door. Her wide smile and deep dimples greeted Lexi. A wave of relief passed over her. Like the night they had first met at the Ashkenaz, Jackie wore her hair natural, pulled back with a thick black headband. Lexi tried to reconcile how cold Jackie had been at the dance club with the warmth of the invitation and the welcome she was experiencing now.

As formal as the outside of the house looked, it was the opposite inside. The hallway was painted a warm burnt orange. Lexi followed Jackie into the living room, here, the walls a light golden brown. Pictures and paintings filled most of the space. Lexi recognized Martin Luther King, Jr. and Nina Simone.

Adding to the warm welcome, there was a small fire in the fireplace. On the mantle, a photograph of who Lexi thought must be Jada. Her hair was braided and, unlike Lexi's fly-aways, Jada's baby hairs along her forehead were smoothed down forming lovely curls along her hairline. "Can I?" Lexi asked, gesturing to the picture.

"May I," Jackie corrected with a nod and a reassuring smile.

Lexi picked up the frame. The Jada in the photo smiled warmly. Robert walked into the room. "She's lovely," said Lexi, returning the photo to the mantle.

"I made an egg bake that will be ready in about ten minutes." Jackie motioned for Lexi to take a seat in a high-backed chair as she and Robert sat on the couch.

"Thank you so much for inviting me, Mrs. Reiger."

"Jackie, please. I'm Mrs. Reiger to my students." Lexi felt as if the sun had just come out. "Coffee or tea?"

"Coffee. Thank you, Jackie." Jackie walked to the kitchen and returned with steaming mugs. Lexi knew from her days working at the bakery that Robert only drank tea. She looked at Robert, "May I call you Robert, Detective?" she teased.

"You'd better. In fact, this had better be the last time you call me "Detective" and the last time you're anywhere near a murder, young lady."

"Speaking of murder, can you talk about the case now?"

He nodded and recounted the progress of the case. Renée's story was that, because she kept pushing Archie's book, David became suspicious and asked if they were having an affair. She panicked, knowing that if David told her husband, he would divorce her and take away everything she loved, mainly the Institute. They argued. Renée insists that David then grabbed her. He pushed her against the door. That was how the hook snapped off.

"She says it was self-defense, but David was hit in the back of the head with the statue. He had to be walking away from her."

Jackie was appalled. "That's awful. How could he? How could she?"

Lexi asked, "Can she claim self-defense?"

"Her lawyer will try. But even Archie knew she was involved somehow and that it had something to do with him. That's why he lied, telling me he'd been paid. He thought that would help Renée. She confessed to the whole thing though."

Jackie shook her head, "That's not love." Reiger and Lexi agreed.

"Was I right about Grey?" Lexi asked.

"You were." Reiger sipped his tea. "His financial records show he'd deposited a $2,000 check just a day before he was killed. He was blackmailing Renée and she felt trapped. She broke into his house and panicked when she couldn't find the negatives. She was there longer than she had planned. He came home. She hid in his office and hit him with the bookend as he came into the room. I don't know if she meant to kill him, she says not. That's when she got very sloppy and grabbed a few books to make it look like a robbery and took off."

"That was one of the things that tripped her up." Reiger continued, "She took the most rare ones. In my experience, people who rob houses don't know anything about books. And, if the thief had been looking to steal rare books, they would have taken the most valuable one. I asked why she left the *Bay Book of Psalms*. She told me she was having an anxiety attack and missed it."

Lexi asked, "So, where are the negatives?"

"Peggy had them in her purse. She had completely forgotten." He shook his head. "It took her days to find them. The negatives were in acetate sleeves and were completely ruined at the bottom of her bag."

Jackie stood up. "That's enough talk of murder. Let's eat."

Over the egg bake and strips of bacon, Robert asked about Lexi's future plans.

"I don't know. I quit the Institute."

He said. "That's a good decision. But what I meant was what does your future look like?"

Lexi was perplexed. "Well, I need a job."

He continued, "Part of growing up is making a family for yourself with friends." He said gravely, "Most people start that process in college. In fact, you should think about going to college."

Lexi laughed. "Okay, Detective. You've figured out my life."

"I'm serious. If you don't imagine anything for your life, it will go by without a thought or direction. No purpose. Is that what you want?"

Feeling on the spot, she remembered the book in her bag. "I have something for you, Jackie." She pulled out a signed first edition of Zora Neale Hurston's *Their Eyes Were Watching God.* She said, "This is from Peggy Neville, Grey's wife. She wanted it to go to a deserving home. She's selling the rest of Grey's collection."

Jackie's face lit up as she took the book and carefully opened it.

After breakfast, they returned to the living room. Lexi saw a photo album on the coffee table and asked if she could look through it.

"Sure," Robert and Jackie said in unison.

Together they looked through photos of Jada as Lexi heard stories about their little girl. She listened to the love expressed by parents who had lost a child as only a child who had lost her parents could appreciate.

THE END

EPILOGUE

Renée was sentenced to life in prison without the possibility of parole. She and Archie broke up.

As fate or synergy would have it, Jack got a public relations job working for big oil.

After serving no time for attempting to poison her husband, Mrs. Amy Davenport Emerson returned to using her maiden name, Davenport. Soon after, she and Gretchen Stenholm began traveling the world. Speculation about the nature of their relationship continued to appear in the press.

Julia Collins quit The Freedom Institute, checked into rehab, met the love of her life and moved to Brisbane, California. They remained sober for the rest of their days.

Though she was disillusioned by libertarianism, Peggy Neville remained at the Institute and refused to ghost write any more titles. It was her revenge to let the dull and tedious books speak for themselves. She hired Archie as an editor and took over as the Director of Public Relations. Even with a raise, she was paid a fraction of Jack's salary.

Wicked Smith and his band experienced mild success on the punk scene, but his career was cut short; he died of a heroin overdose in his room at a residence hotel in North Beach.

Lexi took a position as a receptionist for an employment agency that placed systems analysts at corporations. The job was exciting for Lexi—it was a new and growing field that recruited and managed the careers of the majority of women programmers working on large mainframe computers for big banks and investment firms.

One night in late June of 1987, Lexi was feeding her beloved cat when she saw the light blinking on her answering machine. Nearly 20 years old now, Saxman Bite still had a healthy appetite so Lexi dished out Saxman's food before checking the message. It was her grandmother with an urgent request to call. Lexi's grandfather Brody had died. The news was not unexpected since her grandparents were in their 90s, but, surprising herself, Lexi burst into tears. She arranged for a

leave from work and bought a ticket to fly to Se-
attle before catching a ferry to Ketchikan to bury
her grandfather.

In the third book in the Lexi Fagan Mystery series,
Sins of the Mother, Lexi discovers the truth about
her parents and the plane crash that killed them.
What she learns will lead her to doubt the official
story classifying it as an accident. She begins to
question everything she thought she knew about
herself and her family. The painful and dangerous investigation that follows when she returns to
Ketchikan could be her last.

ACKNOWLEDGMENTS

Writers often talk of the loneliness of writing. My experience has been the opposite. My family and friends have kept me company throughout the process. I have been warmly embraced every step of the way.

There are so many people to thank for helping me with *Free For All*. First, let me thank my family. My mother, Suzanne, and my sister, Heather, are my first readers. Without their encouragement and support, it would not be possible for me to write another word. I want to thank my sister from another mother, Melissa Geraci-Mitchell and her husband, Jason, for their assistance with investigation techniques and cop terms from the 1980s.

Next, I must give props to my editor, Tatjana Greiner. A dramaturge and editor by trade, Ms.

Greiner's comments and suggestions made the story stronger, the characters deeper and she upped my game beyond what I thought possible. I am grateful for her thoughtful and necessary notes.

Once I had addressed Ms. Greiner's notes, I needed a copyeditor. Luckily for me, my friend Francine Hartman stepped up. She took not one, not two, not three, but four passes of the book. She fixed my grammar, corrected my spelling errors and flagged holes in the plot you could drive a truck through. If you enjoyed *Free For All*, it is in no small part because of Francine's razor-sharp attention to detail.

I want to thank another dear friend, Elizabeth Meeker. She showered me with words of encouragement and is willing to be a reader at any stage in the writing process. It has meant the world to me to have such a loyal, supportive friend.

I would like to give a hearty shout out to all libraries and the Library of Congress. Without these institutions—that are filled with hard-working civil servants—we would be a nation without free access to books. Thank you.

And, last but clearly not least, are my readers. I have been encouraged by fans who have made their eager anticipation of the second book in *The Lexi Fagan Mystery* series known in many wonderful ways. Thank you.

COMING SOON

I n *Sins of the Mother*, the third book in the series, Lexi returns to her hometown of Ketchikan, Alaska, for her grandfather's funeral. While there, she is forced to face the truth about her own parents' untimely deaths 20 years earlier. Lexi begins to suspect it wasn't an accident. As she digs for clues, Lexi questions everything she thought she knew about her family—and herself.

If you haven't read the first book in the series, *Baker's Dozen*, discover how Lexi Fagan, newly arrived in San Francisco, lands a job at McCracken's Bakery. When her lover, firefighter Jerry Stevens, turns up dead in a devastating hotel fire, Lexi has no time to mourn. Homicide detective Robert Reiger discovers Jerry's death was no accident. Caught up in the investigation, Lexi uncovers a secret that just might get her killed.

ABOUT THE AUTHOR

Autumn Doerr is a writer and television producer currently based in Los Angeles, but the Bay Area still holds her heart. "San Francisco is where I grew up," says Autumn. "It's where I became an adult, made lifelong friends and where my family still lives."

Autumn is currently working on the third book in the Lexi Fagan Mystery series, *Sins of the Mother.*

Made in the USA
Monee, IL
03 October 2021

79265441R10163